A
HARD
OLD LOVE
AMONGST
SCAVENGERS

A
HARD
OLD LOVE
AMONGST
SCAVENGERS

DAVID DOUCETTE

thistledown press

Thistledown Press Ltd.
410 2nd Avenue North
Saskatoon, Saskatchewan, S7K 2C3
www.thistledownpress.com

Library and Archives Canada Cataloguing in Publication

Doucette, David, 1966–, author
A hard old love amongst scavengers / David Doucette.

Issued in print and electronic formats.
ISBN 978-1-77187-120-4 (paperback). – ISBN 978-1-77187-121-1
(html). – ISBN 978-1-77187-122-8 (pdf)
I. Title.
PS8557.O7858H37 2016   C813'.6   C2016-905258-3
C2016-905259-1

Cover and book design by Jackie Forrie
Printed and bound in Canada

Thistledown Press gratefully acknowledges the financial assistance of the Canada Council for the Arts, the Saskatchewan Arts Board, and the Government of Canada for its publishing program.

A
HARD
OLD LOVE
AMONGST
SCAVENGERS

My Home

On the bank behind the house is a ledge that seems to have
been designed by nature for no other purpose than to give rest.
That is where Charlie would wait. Charlie was a red fox from
Smokey Mountain, the mountain that bears down upon me
here. One spring day Charlie discovered a man raking gravel in
a steep driveway. He also discovered the ledge. He sniffed the
air here, sat back on his haunches. I retrieved for him a piece
of homemade bread and he chowed it down before lifting and
exiting for his high cover of birch, beech, and maple. "Charlie?
Charlie?" I called. "You like that name because it's yours now."
He didn't look back and I thought I would never see him again.

I would not mind seeing him tonight, for it's evening and
I have had enough of my atlas that sits on the kitchen island,
enough of pinpointing where I have been in this grand old
rickety world, these places that now scare me. How did I ever
get back? Why did I ever go because I never will again? Bring
me a friend, Mount Smoke. Night chugs on like a demon train
and the hard old lonesome hour between dog and the wolf is
here. The fiddle will rouse him, get him down off his cursed
mountain. How about "Coralee's Lament"? Nope. No Charlie
tonight. No Charlie in the trees, no Charlie on the slope, not on
the ledge — nowhere through the good glasses I wear. I clean
the precious lenses, even up the gold wings before climbing to
the ledge and seeing the Gut east and how it shakes hands with

a silent ocean. Up at the head of the harbour the coyotes howl. Their straining necks and planted paws come to mind.

My name is Miles 'Kilometres' MacPherson. I was born in 1961 to a village one thousand strong in northeastern Cape Breton. When I was thirteen our Prime Minister of Canada, Pierre Elliot Trudeau, decided to amend all road signs, and our highways went from miles to kilometres. Our cars had new readings on their speedometers and odometers and, number-wise, our world sped up but in a smooth and even way as all went from miles to kilometres, including my name. Miles became Kilometres, it became Klicks, Klicker, even Klicky before a village consensus settled back on Kilometres. I had to get out; it sent me to university at age seventeen. I wasn't going to let Pierre Elliot rename me. I went away for thirty years, to circumnavigate the globe six or seven times. It's back to Miles.

But, hang on, I hear something — let me break off this stick to protect myself. Ah, it's nothing, but I will use the stick in the climb. I am not possessed of strength I once had. I'm thin, my bones rickety.

"Charlie . . . " I call into the woods in a hand-over-hand whisper that enters the branches like a slow bullet to die away unshot, past these beech, birch, and maple; I have reached the plateau.

It was on this plateau, well above Charlie's ledge, a good hundred feet above, that I cut the mountain ash with my chainsaw and gouged a face in its stump. The artwork stands like a mossy old miner hammered long ago into the belly of the ground.

Nieces and nephews of mine came to visit two summers back. They came as a Chaucerian pilgrimage, one speaking movie directions through a pink pylon a single car might use for emergencies. "You're thin, Miles," said the moms and I turned and asked each kid their names as their moms encouraged responses.

"Who wants to see the Tree Ghost?" I said. "Up on the plateau? He talks in a kind, kind old voice. But only when the sun's almost down. Look, it's almost down. And so he should be starting up rate about now."

The moms looked at each other as a youth registry like you never saw came of eyes asparkle and cheeks aglow. It was impossible for the moms to say no. "Go on," they said, with eyes on me. "We'll stay and drink the tea Miles offered. See this house he built. What's your password, Miles?"

"Password?" I said.

"Go on, for god's sakes!" said the second mom slapping the first's shoulder. "He has no internet! Who — Miles?"

"No internet?" said the first.

"No internet, no TV, he probably has no radio. Do you even have power, Miles?"

"Not much," I said. "Not much at all."

I knew this communication talk was a distraction — pretense, they might call it. The ladies wanted to look around. And they could. I had nothing to hide; a journal was there. But anyone who knows how to keep a journal knows how to hide truth. If you want truth, it's here in my face. And I have been playing poker a long, long time.

This was the dry summer of 2009, and because it was dry, wasps had built their cells underground. As we climbed the slope a size-four sneaker darkened the roof of one such domain, an act that summoned a royal fleet. At shoe removal came the blitzkrieg.

The sound was like a bagged chainsaw, revved, held underwater. I was higher up so it took a moment to discover why the children stood there paralysed. But then screams to high heaven notified me, as did the waltzing wallops of wasps, the tiny electric sanders edgings for cheek and forearm. The wasp has no central command but this militant cloud did not suggest that, this deadly blow of striking dandelion seed.

"... ee! " said a boy.

"... oww!" said a girl.

"AHHHHHH!" said the lot.

"Get out!" I said in a schoolyard yell not used in decades. "Get out! Run like yas never ran! Go! Git!"

Run, you say? You mean like this? Like me, down over the Kicking Horse Pass of a bank here where I catch one boy under one arm, girl under the other, armfuls of kids while I shouted for strays to scram down off the damn hill! Which was exactly what I was doing — scramming down over this cursed-ever-loving bank with young heads and arms and legs and feet, flipping and flapping and flopping like party balloons lost of inflation.

I delivered the first parcels to waiting mothers who were aghast and matronly, well out on the step by now, wearing masks of the carnival — was there in fact this Tree Ghost? Was it murdering my poor, poor children!

"Miles!"

But my lungs were aflame and so I communicated nothing, only acted — leaving what brood I had, turning to ascend, to tramp heavy foot on Charlie's ledge, dig in, climb for bodies.

I was loading up stragglers when a boy tugged my shirt.

"What — what!" I said, turning, seeing a pleading oval of face forever dabbed in amateur oil on canvas. The boy pointed upland, spat a wasp from his lip, touched his eyeglasses.

10

"My father," he said. Who? "My father," he said. "He's allergic."

Who? Oh, Neil. Yes, Neil. He had been parking the van away from the bad turn at the bottom of the driveway and had joined us afterward to enter smack dab into a stirred-up wasp site.

Neil sat on a higher bank, in the woods, downplaying the event like a traffic accident victim thrown from a car but landing intact, waited through a type of shock that had him concerned merely with minutia in life: this wrist to his ear — damn watch thing, need a new battery or what?

A wasp alighted in my ear to crawl quick.

"You stung? — Neil!"

"Stung. Yalp."

"You'll have to wait! You and your son! Go up there with your dad," I said to the boy with the face of a painting. "Shoo away from the bees, kid, I said!" A wasp plugged itself into my neck. "Ah! Up there with your dad, you!"

Oh my, a life once embraced of serenity on a hill has now a young father die in front of his kid. I could only do what I could do. Which was to dash-sneaker these others off the slope.

Oh, the huff, the puff. The Kilometres, with his metric tonne.

"Here," I said to a mom and I turned to call upslope to the bank, to the stranded duo of father and son but with all the wailing going on behind and me without a voice it was pointless. I somehow got back up. The son was okay; the father I edged off the hill like good furniture. Careful with the arms, careful with the legs. And he was inside my house then. As I was in my car, then, the Rocket with its dying transmission, dashing for my neighbor Tim Dickey's for an antidote. "Come, busted transmission!" I slapped the wheel of the Ford GT. "They race these in England," said Shugar Biggs in Toronto who sold it to me. "You got a good car there."

Tim's wife maybe entered a bedroom when I arrived whereas Tim Dickey from his La-Z-Boy said, "Bee sting allergy? Miles, me son! What are you talking epinephrine for — epinephrine isn't an antidote! It stimulates a massive immune response! Try it, though, I could be wrong. Here."

Young parent Neil sat in my purple chair by my favourite window, daylight making him grim-grey forever. Yet he breathed. A hysterical mom shifted weight and blew hair from her face, her child's pleas undying.

Oh, my quiet room, my lonesome house — its middle floor assailed with alerts and confusions; I saw salt tracks on the little faces. Were they ever going to ease up?

But then there was this falling off, this "ah", a general silence even before one great utter renewal of misery originating in the youngest whelp began.

"Yes!" I answered the prosecution. "*Yes, what had happened was terrible! Yes, I am to blame! Yes, I do see welts big as twenty-five cent pieces!*"

"We're concerned about who else might be allergic"? said a brave mom, her counterpart nodding. "Because we don't know if one of the kids is or not! You, and this cursed house on this damn hill they all had to see!"

I sat through that. I stood through it. I saw stings settled like pock on young arm, face, and neck. Which is when a kid pointed and said, "Bee!" A blue-murder wailing to outdo all prior came. I'll lose my hearing in this, music's done for me, I thought. I looked out the window expecting to see the cops come. Silent houses sat in pretty rows across the water along the Woody Shore.

Daddy-o Neil in my favourite chair waited placid. Pallid — I mean to say; I've had zero handle on vocabulary since I got back. Was Neil drifting from this world to that?

The sight of an antihistamine wielded by one of the moms brought calm. A reasonably bitten kid had retrieved it from their van's glove compartment. Kids — redheads, blonds, blacks, brunettes; all sniffed out sorrow to see the action. For as Odysseus said of mourning, for his deceased dad — you grow tired of it.

An all-calm worked itself into the living room and distress eased. Which is not to say a macabre sight and sights did not prevail. The spectacled boy at his allergic dad's knee looked up; innocent eyes focused, fists got balled, a face reddened.

"Dad?"

"What?" said Neil. " — What?"

"You were crying."

"No, I wasn't." The gang blew apart in laughter. "I wasn't!"

I thought the roof would lose her moorings in the gales of laughter. But all were safe, none maimed, none scarred — I hope — and what a story. A smile came even to my lips. To have a family must be a good thing; all the company you have along the way. Reassured mothers squared happy heads, pointed faces for the door. "All right, you gang! Blow it to the car!"

That night, after I got the house back, with my pot of soup on the woodstove top behind the flue, I grabbed the old eleven-dollar guitar and stomped and sang "My Home".

> *Oh take me back*
> *And leave me be*
> *Where my friends*
> *All wait for me*
> *And it's you*
> *I'll not leave*
> *You I'll not grieve*
> *My home, my home, my home.*

Above the Rocky Shore

The first winter back I woke to baying but not the long-off, up the head of the harbour type. I went down to the icy second floor and looked through the French doors, through windows with no curtains nor their prospect and I saw a company of coyotes circle my house counter-clockwise. These usually work in pairs but a family may stay together in a pack. I might have had garbage in the basement, which they caught scent of. You had to careful of habituation; the males got up to fifty pounds. One paused to register the effect of their procession on me. He panted, kept his marble eye fixed before trying again the snow before him. He trotted, rejoined the prison-yard circle.

Glass was between us. We met as climates, of darkness and cold confronted with, well, some light, some heat. Their eyes were a glazed grey and their pelts wore snow. I had nothing for fending off these cats at the fish bowl but then I remembered the .410 shotgun and I went above to the storage nook. My brother had broken into the house and hidden this gun back in the Chrétien days when a national gun registry debate was on. I had no shells but I took it down and held it up to the coyotes. Tongues lolled, vapours drifted from open mouths. "Here, sister to the wolf! See what I got!" One eyed me, as if to say, "But no shells, eh? Glass helps you this time, maybe light too, to become your tortoise shell. But, dweller. Remember this face."

The gold glasses? How do they figure in? These that bring sharpness to an Acadian forest slope? The glasses come from around the Salt Lake, from the old homestead where I grew up. They were jammed down in between the gyprock and the china cabinet in the cold room where I slept as a boy. I was rummaging over there after I came back to the Island and I said right off the bat, "These'll do." My eyes had badly weakened over there and I had done little about it since returning. Too far from civilization to address it, I would conclude, though Sydney was only an hour away. Perhaps it was Smokey Mountain, the great geographical barrier that had always made this place feel so cut off. The slipping transmission in the Rocket? No, it was me. I was not interacting.

I remember looking at my reflection in the china cabinet after I found them. Ha, maybe the look of the scholar's your aim? Nope — seeing's my aim and yet something in their wearing did speak of a lone man on a quiet hill looking better in antique eyewear. I could see little with this set, of course, their prescription having long been assigned to another. To whom, the other? God only knew. I was just a grey-headed ghost haunting his childhood home.

I took the glasses in to Dr. D. R. Labelle in Sydney to have them installed with proper lenses. "Light," he said of their weight, "though sturdy. Let's have a look your eyes. You'll feel a puff of air here. Your mother had glaucoma, you say? Well, you do have a stigma. In your left eye."

"Is it bad?"

"It's common."

"My right is okay?"

"You'll need glasses." He looked at me here. "Your eyes have deteriorated. You've been a while without proper nutrition." It was one of those question-statement question-statements.

"Who? Me? Oh, no. I'm good."

Labelle was the only one in this crowded second-storey shop not to wear glasses. He wore jeans, a long-sleeve denim shirt, leather loafers.

"I went to Nepal with Doctors Without Borders," said Dr. D. R.

"Do Doctors Without Borders need passports?"

"What I needed was to fill a lot of heavy prescriptions. Yes, I needed a passport." And then in what seemed confidence he said, "Watch out for eyesight in the poor." His eyes were glassy green, little hoods were over the pupils. Ah ha! Contacts.

"Why in the poor?" I said. "Look for the eyesight?"

"*Because* is why."

This had been a favourite answer of my mother's. But this doctor without a border, D. R. Lapelle, had told me much. His sharing of his Nepal experience resulted from an assumed fellowship — he had gleaned for our conversation that I too had travelled. I believe he had prior knowledge.

He put a few drops in my eyes that turned the world into a water place. He had me select frames from a wall rack.

"Second pair's free," he said, perhaps for the thousandth time in his entrepreneurship. I felt the rack, felt what seemed to be decent frames. Not big, not small, smooth.

I drove my car in the street and remarked, "Why, look at the all the other cars down here at fifty fathoms." I was wearing the free pair, which I'd lose before the week was out. I don't know why they let me leave in this state. I suspected I was having an adverse reaction. My antique pair were being fitted with lenses adhering to specifications of my prescription. They were to be dipped in gold that cleaned them, they said, their missing nose-bridge pad installed. One week, they said. Come pick them up then. Oh I will do just that — if that sign indeed says Exit and not Stop.

It was deep autumn and I leaned on a rake. I turned to see, through brass-coloured birch leaves, the fall of my driveway. But I heard something. Someone was climbing the hill, crunching its gravel. I took a couple steps to see past the apple tree of mid-slope. My father, on his first visit to the house that took me seven years to build — he was tackling the terrain.

"Hello, Dad!"

He waved. "Stay with your work, Miles!"

I put down my rake. Someone must have let him out at the road. That must have been the door I thought I had heard. But my father closes doors gently. I learned the habit from him and it was a practice that had served me well, one I also applied to many things. The man never knew the word no. He was like the Japanese I met; they'd avoid no at all costs. My father was eighty-one but climbed well.

I met him at the apple tree and took his overnight bag. I took his arm too, a slim delicate appendage possessed of strength, yes, but tender old age. We weren't a touching family but with much of life gone, for all of us, that habit had to die.

"You crept up on me like a fox, Dad."

"Ho, ho!" he said. "Miles? Where'd you get those? I remember those."

He was staring at me and his eye contact had me look away. "The glasses?" I said,

"Yes, the glasses. They were mine. I got a piece of metal in my eye in 1957. They suit you rate well."

"You want them back?"

"Heavens, no! I have two or three pairs here in my shirt pocket." He did not touch the pocket because he needed all his balance to climb. He had me stop, to look at the harbour and the ocean. He caught his breath.

"I found them in the old house," I said.

"You did?" he said, turning, coming back to the topic. "Ha! I can't get over it seeing you in those."

"Why is that?"

"Because I thought you would never age, Miles. Though you're thin."

He was the youthful one, coming all this way from Halifax, his clear blue eye flashing on me, on the land, the house, his old property across the water.

"I found them in the old cold room over there," I said as we closed in on the house.

"Where you learnt your guitar. I remember. No, you wear those. They're all yours now. Things must be sharper."

"Really sharper."

"Sharper's what you want."

We got to the step and I set his bag down.

"Holy hell! Look at that mountain bearin' down on ya," he said. "And that ledge there. It looks like a seat, like nature designed it to be nothing else. You never did catch anything, Miles? In all those countries you were to? Illness?"

"I was lucky, Dad."

"Well, all that's done now, hear? Miles? No, let's not go in the house not rate yet. I've been in that automobile all the hell the way down the highway and my legs need a free minute. Leave the bag, no animal will get at the ham and cheese sandwich I got in there. Ah my. The air's what forgot. The sweetness."

"That's what I felt. It always was the air here."

"That's what your mother said, too. Look at the house you built! Holy Heavens! I raised that big gang over there across the water and had nothing like this. You must be glad to be in it."

"I owe."

"Oh, owe — we all owe. You have. Have's the thing."

"I don't know what I have, Dad."

"Back is what you have. You're in your home, free, healthy, alive. You have everything there is to have. Just get some weight on your bones. You look like Humphrey Bogart."

We burned spruce brush that afternoon and its black billows curled down over the bank to choke off the Cabot Trail. "See the way the smoke goes?" said my father. "This curling off the mountain. That's what you'll get in your flue." We laughed at how cars entered the smoke mash only to creep out the other side, with a driver clutching a wheel, a passenger digging a knuckle in the dash — both expectant of the big bang. Their not seeing how little their danger was made the joy.

"Glasses would hardly help in that soup," said my father as he twisted his head in the way he had always twisted it in confirmation. He nodded at a remote thought; I did the same. We were travellers, him and me. Travellers who lounged on a rake and a shovel out in the sun, peering through a general heat for the crackling flames of a smoky brush fire.

"For the love of God — Miles! Liven this place up!" said my father. "Get out that old flea market guitar out and heave away on her!" We had been out on the deck north in the dark and had heard the pain of the coyotes at the head of the harbour. We sat at the table.

"I don't play a lot," I said.

"Who — you? Well, change that! You got to keep it together down here. I only came to see you were. Give us a little of that Rocky Shore song of yours. I'll play along on the violin."

"I thought you didn't play anymore."

"Not when the opportunity's here. Promises like that are for when things are dead. This old fiddle? She survived that big gang of kids."

"The kids were nothing . . . "

"What — compared to where you had it? I suppose, she's had some travels with you, all right."

"You didn't want it hung on a wall. Remember?" He wasn't listening. He surveyed the instrument.

"She's all full of glue or something. And coming apart here. Where'd ya have her?"

"Oh, I'm cleaning her up. Bit by bit, just so with a dab of alcohol here and there."

"Too bad we didn't have a dab of alcohol. Was it you who said it was from 1894?"

"That's what the symphony guy in Brazil told me."

"I got it from an old fellow who used to come to the house when I was eleven years old. She was in the same shape then as she is now. You can't kill her, I guess." He put it on his shoulder. "Not the music, anyhow." He tried a note. He had me promise to play this violin when my mother died. The feeling for it had left from his hands, he said that day.

"Let's get at her, Miles."

So with my old man on fiddle again the night got closed out with a stomp at the eleven-dollar guitar. We played "Above the Rocky Shore".

A Hard Old Love Amongst Scavengers

So green the grass
Of Middlehead
Where the seabirds
Fly overhead
A bright blue bay
The rolling farms
I have you here
You're lying in my arms.

Every Night at My Window

One spring day, watching my bearings because I hadn't erected railings, I stepped out on the deck east. It was early in the construction and I slept with building materials. No — layers of fiberglass insulation do not make a blanket. No, a folded layer does not make a pillow even if you wrap it in a sweater. My skin would be itchy forever. I had taken on far more than I could handle with this house but the view from the deck east was wide and bright and a freshness from the sea rose to meet me in the sun. No leaves were on the trees but finally warmth had come. I had on a red T-shirt, and because of the long solitary work up here I was hale.

I sucked in air and surveyed torn earth, the work of the excavator. No primary colors showed on the wasted soil and the slate-grey fiberglass wrap worn by the house hardly had the property looking like a flower patch. A whirring was at my ear, then my chest. A hummingbird, having seen my red shirt, drilled at my breastplate. I took two swats and he flew past my head at a million miles an hour for the window east. And the bird, sure that the transparency there was just another bit of air to fly through, hit the pane with a *thawp*. I went below, lifted its limp body from dead grass. He stared at me then flew smack off up in through the balcony door I had left open.

Inside, high, high above, like a monstrous housefly, he buzzed. He was at the summit window, tapping there. Ah, my. No upper floor existed yet so I set an old wood ladder from the homestead against a wall. On top of this I placed a stepladder. On this I set a sawhorse — lengthways, topping all off finally with a bucket of paint. I was up twenty-seven feet and could almost reach him when he flew twelve inches higher. I had seen a man in the Taiwanese circus climb a tower of cups and saucers. I got on tiptoe; with my T-shirt light over my hand I nabbed him.

Down on the floor, with him in my shirt, I looked up at the ladders. "I will be definitely kilt here yet."

I took him out on the deck. "You sure are green, Hum Machine. Can't say I felt a heart beat like yours. What kind of heart is it? An electrical-shock heart? Free as a bird, then. Sing your way back to Ireland on a good green leprechaun wing, I'll play you, 'Crossing to Ireland' on the fiddle tonight."

I opened my hand. He didn't fly.

"Not so easy. Is it? Freedom restored."

He left me, soared into a morning sun for all mountains west, for places not so bright yet ones that gave access to a whole sky to enter into and twist about.

At six the next morning, humming and tapping came to the windows. The humming and tapping found me at last where I wrote my journal in good light. It was him, the green hum machine.

"What, bird? Never thought we humans could set something free? Often we can't. Breaks our hearts too bad."

Every morning that bird came, checking out all the curtainless windows to find where I was. He made a summer of it.

It was the precious last two weeks in October when the leaves wait ablaze for the half-week of rain and wind to remove them from where they're bound. My father was visiting before winter set in and the house was virtually habitable after all these years of building. I had one thing left to ask him, about the war. It was just the two of us and the fall wind elbowed me to whisper: "Go on, Miles. Ask him. Take the opportunity that soon won't be yours."

"I don't talk about that!" said my old man, warming himself by a brushfire we had going on the higher flat. He was telling me the wood I was handling was too heavy for me, that I would hurt myself up here all alone. That I had to go easy because I was not as strong as I was. "But with all respect, to your mother . . . " he said.

"What's that?" I said, out from under brush.

"There was someone over there and when we all went back for the fifty-year liberation ceremony the other year back I entered a phone booth. She was there in the book."

"Alive?" I was carrying a big tree. I set it down.

"Yes, alive, I saw her. I spent the night."

"You what?"

"On her couch, why not? Your mother was gone. Her husband was gone. Her kids gone. But she didn't want to make a go of it."

"And you did?"

"I can't really say."

"Probably best."

"I believe that." His blue eyes skipped over the fire, over the harbour for the Gut. He looked at Middlehead where clouds had sat the whole afternoon.

"All those years," I said to him. "You the father of a big family. Always with my mother. Devoted Always a little love in there, eh, don't tell me. Is that how the heart operates?"

"'Tis a fact. All have a little love down there. A lot gets played out down there. You might not think it does."

"Let's go to the harvest."

On the built-up field we harvested my garden and got enough to fill the front of my old man's outstretched T-shirt.

"A good stew is here," he said and we trudged back up to the house. Near the top he dropped a zucchini grown to the size of a golf ball and it rolled bit by bit to mock us. Or me, the farmer.

After the stew my father said, "Give us a tune, Miles, for the love of God. It feels like the power's out here in ones of those big storms to hit when you fellas were all young. Shake the walls. Do you remember where we got that little guitar of yours?"

"Do I?" I said bringing it from below the kitchen island. "I'd have paid the twenty." We had been at the old Halifax Forum and an old woman was selling this tiny busted guitar for twenty bucks.

"Will you take fifteen?" I had asked her.

"What's the tag say?" she said. She had to make me say it.

"Twenty," I said.

"Then twenty it is."

I told my father and he said, "Leave it to me." I looked for him everywhere at the flea market's end but because he was so short and had always blended into any scene I had to wait till nearly every soul disappeared. I saw him, he carried the guitar.

"Twenty?" I said.

"Eleven. There's one thing you got to learn, Miles. Charm, charm will get ya right through life."

He left for Halifax and I climbed past skeletal beech. The thing about visitors is they leave you lonesome when they go. White and yellow birch were above now, green moss on grey stone below; brass sarsaparilla too for my golden rims. With

25

eyewear the world clears as it does when you put a glass-bottom bucket on stirred water. My neighbour Tim Dickey gave me the gift of this homemade stick. It was too heavy for my hand so I used it as a fire poke. The fire sharpened its end then dried it bottom-up to make it light. Coyotes were no threat; I didn't worry about the bear. But to have something in the hand was good. Moose go crazy. They get a meningeal worm. Once I saw a gorgeous black bear babbling to itself way up in these here stubborn trees. Its ball and pad were imprinted in the clay for a week.

There was scratching and I turned to see nothing. Why? Because it came from above. A downy woodpecker was atop a beech. He tried his beak in the bark and then rotated around the trunk as if on a carousel. "I know why you're here, Downy. Because that little head is possessed of knowledge." Another arrived and the pair came along. I could hear a red-tailed hawk click high above. "Companionship for protection? That your game? Come then lovers, follow."

At the top of the mountain was a flat area that often held a pond. The weather had to be overly wet. Garret Doyle travelled up here with me once.

"How fragrant," he said.

"What is?"

"The fir."

"What fir?"

He then pointed out a beautiful batch of Christmas trees and from then on I learned to smell the woods. "Here," I had said to Garret that day. "The place I told you about. But dry as a bone today."

"Look how the treetops leave a circle for the sky. Maybe this was a meeting place. Feels like a cradle."

And so Cradle it became. But both those guys are gone, Garret Doyle and Dad. Long gone from the mountain and from here. So what am I doing here? All alone atop the hill in a big house across from where I was born? And I have been further than those guys could ever have dreamed. Singing is what. Stomping at the old eleven-dollar guitar to "Every Night at my Window".

> *Every night at my window*
> *I look down at the dark road*
> *That climbs to the house upon the hill*
> *I think I see you coming*
> *But that's just the darkness running*
> *To surround the house*
> *Where you and I did live.*

Going To See My Maker

I couldn't stop looking at the ants. I had no ride back to Sao Paulo and the horse veterinarians had all gone home drunk from the afternoon *feijoada*, a bean and beer party. There was a tryst I remember but something happened. A woman had slapped me and left me on the bleachers at the riding grounds. The paddock was empty but the sun shone. A small smart dog they kept around the stalls to chase out rats was my company. He knew I was destitute and so sat alongside.

I saw the ants, each with a huge piece of leaf carried vertically on its back. And though it's a strange sentence, their work created silence. One by one by one by one they marched, each with a leaf section along their erratic trail, alone but together along this drunkard's path without hesitation. What was good was that I did not try to understand the business of it. The sun was warm on my shoulders and with my heel I eased my fiddle case out of its direct light. I patted the dog and asked him his name. I could smell the hay and the manure and the soap they washed the Thoroughbreds with. I heard a dripping hose.

It was not going to be cold, I was a guy, I knew many words of Portuguese to disarm any bandits. And my fiddle could always disarm. Until they walked off with it, maybe. Off in the distance was a city of twenty million and I had to get into it. I saw the thin drunkard who had finished his stall cleanings, who had purchased his bottle of *cachasa* and now lay paralyzed at the dirty grass. He would see the sunrise. But he was no gringo. Someone or something would get me back to the tiny house with the bars on the window where I lived in the garden of a Sao Paulo millionaire. Right now were the Brazilian ants. The biting Brazilian ants.

I stood at the Cradle. The pond was still as glass and it mirrored the stirring autumn leaves enough to think you could walk the surface. A shiver went through as wind passed overhead. On his last climb to the top of the mountain my father took me here. "Don't buy this land. There's nothing here for the likes of you. You're a wanderer, Miles. This is land for someone without ambition."

It is people who know you best that know you least. I had no ambition and then he moved a bush and I saw the glorious valleys of the head of the harbour stretch for mountains west. We both hushed in witness to the arteries, to these Highlands where blood flowed to a criminally dark land.

"I see clear cross to Mongolia," I said.

"Those are some eyes, to see that far. I can't even pronounce that. I see the harbour."

Today was warm in the sun, my sharp stick giving me balance. I got down on moss under a pine. Every blow up here, every drop of rain, every snowflake to fall and to settle — that's what this forest knows. I picked a blueberry. "The land, up here, is what this place is," I had told my father. "Is there anything for anyone anywhere?" He didn't answer because there is no answer. Then he said, "Home is what's for people. I don't know if it is home. If you're all alone."

From the moss and through prescription glasses I saw straight to the ravine where a high-flying eagle fell a full two seconds before swooping up like a roller coaster for more of the fun. It was probably five hundred metres to that other side where in a fall woods came the slow crackle of footfall. It was a red fox, piloting through the downed leaves. He was all alone travelling this backcountry, the rest of creation erased for him as if by pencil. I whistled a long note and his four legs stiffened, his face and neck aimed like a rifle. His eyes then found mine. But that long bushy tail what's the purpose there beyond adding beauty? Swatting flies maybe. He twisted away and picked up speed and I watched him till he tired on the upper ridge. They say man can run down any animal. I heard crackle of paw in leaves then saw no more.

I was trying to note the eighths of an inch on a measuring tape when I realized my gold glasses were gone. Ripping chipboard, my Skilsaw spat vicious chips at my face. The glasses had offered protection, too. Now where the old hell were they?

I searched the house high and low, pausing at photographs or to try on clothes I had not worn. They were especially big in the shoulders and wrists. I'd then remember what had brought me up to the third floor and say, "Get on with it! Find your glasses!"

I called up Tim Dickey. He was repairing his lobster traps and drinking.

"I lost my glasses, Tim."

"Ah, me son, ya don't mean to say, not your old man's — Miles! They're precious, bai. Where'd you lose thum?"

I touched my toque, folded my arms against the cold in the house. "Now there's a bright question."

"You know what I mean. Where'd you have them on last?"

"The mountain. I had them on when I saw that fox. I searched the house high and low only to discover one thing."

"What's that?"

"That you only get a couple of shots at finding something because you soon keep forgetting what it is you're looking for."

"Did you try the glove compartment?"

"I will."

"Can't be easy looking for a thing that gives you vision. I'll come up."

"Can you drive?"

"Nope."

"Drinking?"

"Yes. But I got no license."

"I'll phone you tomorrow if I can't find them."

I put down the cold phone and looked down at my car. It sat on the built-up field where I was too lazy to go down to. Someone had a fire on across the harbour. Maybe I gave them the idea to burn. It's all I wanted to do, burn. I was always cold.

Tickety Tim they called Tim Dickey. When he was young he used to get lots of speeding tickets. Tickety Tim Dickety's a better name. Tim started making walking sticks right after losing his license for drinking and driving. I never knew him to drive fast. He came to help that day. We searched till the snow fell.

It was spring and Tim and I headed up over the hill with his sticks. He showed me new detailing up around the grip. His plan for the summer was to sell the sticks around the Cabot Trail, he had fifty in his basement. He hadn't gotten along with his wife over the winter so he'd had the time.

There was no sign of the glasses going up the hill. We had been hopeful because in spring, all terrain is tamped down.

At the Cradle, the day being warm, the winter having been long, Tim wanted to get in the water. We got down to our boxers and entered it.

"Well, Jesus!" he said. "Look! Snow in the woods yet and we're in here!"

"I told you that!"

"Any man's a boy, I guess. Here's one now with pneumonia."

I think he was hung over and that's why he wanted to go in. We got dressed and with chattering teeth crouched to see a four-toed salamander. Tim saw it better than I did. The creature lay still, waiting for the temperature to go above freezing.

"It'll be a while for that," said Tim.

"They breathe through their skin and have no lungs."

"I won't either, after this pneumonia sets in."

"Is that four toes on the hind feet? Should be."

"I won't have any, if we don't get off this hill."

"Bai, it was you who wanted to go in!"

"Yeah, well, anything but temptation I can resist. Let's get below to that fire of yours 'fore a man freezes rate slap bang to det. My teeth, listen, near rocked outta me head!"

"Could you have a look, Tim? On the branches on the way down? They might have gotten snarled in a limb."

"I looked, in the limbs. I looked in the leaves. Combed every bough with both me eyeballs. Studied roots. Studied crowns, for some stupid reason. I looked and looked till I got a left, then a right eye near put out! Three or four occasions! They're gone, me son! Leave them gone! We were up here all last fall, then this winter in snowshoes. You got me and everyone else in the community dreaming of them! Them and them Tree Ghosts of yours!"

At the bottom, standing on the deck north peering across the harbour where a fire on the shore burned, Tickety Tim

Dickety told me of his painful relationship. He mentioned a girlfriend.

"You're married, Tim, I thought. Was it her I met when I went for the bee salve?"

"You oint listening. Miles! Yes, it's her but, me son! You got glasses on the brain! I don't want to talk anymore about her."

I didn't pursue it. I had been away. I poured Tim a shot of whiskey from a bottle someone had fired in the ditch below. I wouldn't have any myself and he went along with this like a gentleman. Not all alcoholics do. Tim's face turned beet-red before his lips met the glass. In a second he was drunk and talking like a man released from a dungeon. "Oh me, oh my, Miles, I'm glad, glad, glad you're home but that's it for me. You check your clothes, Miles? Pockets? You said they were slim."

He patted his hair and I could see he was losing it — because he was trying to grow it and this only highlighted the regions where it used to grow.

"Six times, Tim. Each pocket. I told you. You only get a few shots at finding what's lost. You have to pay attention at the start of your search, after that they could be right there and you can't see them. Only when you aren't looking do you have a chance. Ten years down the road, maybe, they'll surface. They were lost to begin with."

"That's what I kept saying. Some things are meant to be lost. I'm lost."

I wasn't paying attention; I rubbed a shirt pocket, rubbed a pants pocket. I would check the glove compartment after he left. It was obsession. Spring was here and I wanted to get at the road I had started in the fall. It would be good to have those glasses for that.

"Memory's shot, Tim."

"It was all those travels, Miles. That spicy food. You need a break, me son. A break one year won't fix, not for someone like you. You're so full of the road you got ditches on both sides of ya. Yes, hard, hard winter. I near lost it myself."

Glove compartment, I told myself, write that down. Yes, mania because that which is not in our lives due to our negligence drives us battiest of all. One old fellow in Sydney told me to get a wife if I kept losing things, though there was no ring on his finger.

"Nothing's ever really lost," said Tim, drawing me back to his topic, using philosophy.

"My glasses are, fool."

He got quiet then, poor Tickety Tim Dickety. Oh, poor Timothy Middle-Name Dickety, how I maybe broke your heart with that word and how you would break mine with that deed. We're together and apart, eh, Tim? And can only hear our own voices.

Loss. Old Eleven knows it. Every song I knew knew it. I closed the door on that night with "Going to See My Maker".

> *When you gonna leave*
> *My woman?*
> *Is it gonna be today?*
> *Well, I wish you well*
> *My woman*
> *For there a journey*
> *I also gotta take.*

No glasses turned up. I searched the summer, the fall, and the winter like a man possessed. As a side project I worked on the road, till the rough weather came. But the finding of those glasses was the main project. I mapped out the mountain, carried a leaf rake with me, priced metal detectors. When winter laid itself out and snow blanketed the ground I was sure a white world this second time would highlight gold on a branch, because things die, spots open. No luck. It was spring then, before the green, all tamped down and I called Tim.

"Dry in the woods, Tim."

"Dry is it."

"What do ya say to a little mountain trek?"

"Look. I've had it with these let's-look-for-your-lost-granny-glasses tramps!"

"All right, then."

"Okay. For you. But straight up, my ankles can't take a meander."

"Straight up, Tim, I promise. Pond's full."

"She is is she? Because she can be full all she wants to be. Caught couple year's worth of pneumonia from that last time. Oh. Ah, Miles?"

"Yeah?"

"Nothing. Give me ten minutes."

He arrived by bicycle. He had wanted to ask me something. Perhaps the hike would bring it out. It did not. And we had no luck with the glasses.

We lost touch after that. "We" — I say? I, I mean. I drifted away as I am prone to do from folk that comprise family and friends. It's not an anti-social reaction I don't think. I just forget. Forget that keeping people in the picture is what you must do. But no — you wander the hill, Miles. Farther and farther afield of care and disappointment in others. Free of those towers of guilt we all build. Get up over Smokey where the towers are below. Where treetops sweeten the air and underfoot is a dry leaf, and all about, unbreakable loneliness.

It was the second year and giving up was my plan. My father's golden glasses were gone and in my journal I wrote a two-word entry: "Leave be." Yet — the glint of sun on the harbour, the striking of fool's gold on my road, and my mind leapt back to the project. Because how great it would be to find them! Stop, for love of God, stop. Forget your glasses — it's been a trip a day up that cursed mountain for these twenty-four months. If they're there they're buried. You've seen how earth climbs a windfall to eat it.

It was the kitchen calendar I studied, the month of September, there was a pumpkin scene with a young family in scarves and good boots. But please tell me to God this is not 2010 and that this much of life is gone?

Geese honked on the cold mornings. They flew the length of the harbour seaward, honking to beat hell, honking for anything and everything to get out of the damn way — despite clear sailing, as far as my eye could see. Baby 1 and Baby 2 of the eagles clucked and soared at dawn down over the hill above their talon-scrapped pine. Their quiet heads had at last quit the nest, I guess, after a long time of stretching wings — to check these things out. The whole family watched the harbour in the evenings, settled in as if for TV. My finances laid me low.

I called the University College.

"Isn't that something 'cause we were just about to call you, Miles. Someone needs to save us. Can you design an English course? Something about Cape Breton? The foreign community's growing and we have two hundred students. Is Halloween a possible finish? . . . What's that? . . . Music? I guess so."

I called the University Press.

"We have three manuscripts in need of opinions. Fifty-buck stipend, apiece."

I called the Royal Canadian Legion in North Bay.

"Music? Not really, Miles. How are your siding skills?"

The siding brought home the bacon and I would make it till Christmas. I could then vanish back into the larger world to play music and teach English. I had convinced myself of this, in any case. In reality I would never go out there again.

I flipped the phonebook shut and turned for the open balcony door where beyond a Great Blue Heron struggled in a harbour flight. Like a poopy child, it came, alone, low, working wings to offset a drop from the sky.

Crispness cut over the woodpile out back as I bent to gather a few sticks. Oh, my back. Now where did that come from? Am I that brittle, that ready to break? I am just not bouncing back. But why should it be otherwise? A time comes when bouncing back is no longer the case. I had not gained back the weight, that's for sure. I didn't like people thinking I was sick.

I worked at the driveway, digging for bedrock onto which I laid the concrete tracks. Into a wet mix I twisted flat pieces of pink granite, as surfacing. I went in the Rocket to gather these stones from Smokey. The apple tree was halfway from road to house. I contemplated a switchback here, before the run to the top. This road to me was the borrowed one hundred and fifty thousand dollars, the bank paper I signed during my years over wherever the hell I was. The borrowed money seemed always to rush straight down the road like water from an overfilled tub, spilling onto the Cabot Trail, then over the bank to the harbour. I couldn't look at it sometimes from the house. Deflect it, I told myself, bury its steepness halfway in a curve at the apple tree. Get that crazy Feng Shui going. You should know about that, you were over there. Straight roads are suspect, straight never the way it is. Twist, turn, bend — slow that blood money down, man!

I picked, I raked. I shovelled and got my thin arms going to fill in the wheelbarrow. I had eaten a good dish of porridge today so I wasn't hungry. But someone watched and I turned.

"Hi, Charlie. Can't stay away, eh? It's been awhile."

It was my plan to get him used to me so I stepped down the road, watching him of course out of the corner of my eye. He sat on his haunches, but away from his ledge. He was on a closer bank, right where the juncos had hatched. Could it be he needed company? I entered a dip in the built-up field, the same field I had carried thirty wheelbarrow-loads a day to for a year and a half; six to nine feet of vertical of brush lay buried here.

I passed out of sight and went fast around the back of the house where I slipped in the back door and in the kitchen grabbed a hunk of homemade bread. I had been alone; people knew I had gone crazy looking for my glasses and so they stayed away — that was one reason. It was fall. Company would be good.

I tossed the bread and the startled fox leapt for high cover.

"Get back down here! Charlie! Charlie!"

I returned to my pick and to banging bedrock. I went to get my shirt at the apple tree and a limb scraped my neck, the limb from the last time Tim Dickey was here. He had just got his license back and came to show me his new paint job on that wreck of a truck he drove. While backing down, the limb had caught and scraped the passenger side of his truck like a flathead screwdriver held in the strong fist of a mean man. Tim knew not to come for damages; I fought the church mice for crumbs.

"People get hurt up here," I had told him. "Those kids, the bees. Now, damaged vehicles. I need to install a no-visitors sign at the road."

Tim didn't find this clever. And Tim Dickey would never come for damages. I had committed the worst of sins. A sin we all commit. Not to see the good around us. His visits were good. I left my road and its work and headed up. My father was in the hospital. That was on my mind. It had been on my mind when Tim was up.

Conditions were such that voices travelled like they were coming from next door. A draft left the mountain to come over my head and work itself down for the harbour. It caressed air there yet there was no ripple. They could hear me over there tonight. Why do I know? Because I could hear them. I could hear their plain-spoken conversation. I listened to see if my name came up. But maybe the sound is one way and they cannot hear me. In any case, I went easier tonight, closing out the day with a stomp at the eleven-dollar guitar of "The Rocky Shores of Ingonish".

> *Oh, stay with me always*
> *In these Highlands by the sea*
> *Where our gentle hearts*
> *Will always somehow*
> *Make ends meet.*

A Part of the Sea

There's a moose here called MacIntosh and he's the biggest creature you ever want to meet. I saw him one spring evening as the sun hit the bad turns of the ski hill. I was running at the time and needed exercise like a fish needs a swim, but I would socialize this way, waving at cars and their drivers at me. When the bad turns ended I saw the half-mile of shallows where the clam-flats do not take sun. Three moose beyond were in a sparkling sun, two bulls and a cow. The bulls fought for their prize and I saw them fall in the water and turn brown pelts over in splashes that came high as houses. They resurrected. Their kicks glistened and water rolled from shook antlers. The larger, driving off the adversary, was MacIntosh. MacIntosh eats apples in the fall by folding his front legs and getting down as if to pray in church.

I have a friend on the slope tonight. We meet again.

I was playing "Keats' March" on the deck north above the harbour and opened my eyes to a tiny red light below. It was through the birch, across the road, it was the light of a deck hatch where a band of boaters clapped and whistled for more. There was a splash and I retreated, crossing the floor to ensure the back door to the bank was locked. Just before I touched off the switch that lit up the maw of the bank, I saw Charlie on his ledge. "Ho, here we are!" At my cupboard I ripped off a hunk of bread.

"Now don't go squandering," I said out on the step into night air. "I squandered and look where it got me." That made little sense. I had a house, I had a car; yet there was squandering. "You better like it, that's my mother's recipe." He turned his head away. "Oh, I thought it was cats vain like that. Do you like the ledge nature scrapped off for you? I got one too."

Charlie might have been there an hour listening to my fiddle. The sound might have pulled him down off the mountain the way it had pulled these boaters with the tiny red light in below the birches. I tossed underhanded. Hansel and Gretel pieces climbed to him. "Come now, that's good bread and I ain't going to waste much more of it! Eat that, I said!"

He left the bank then, approached a morsel out on the ground and, with the most delicate of manner, bent and took a pinch in his jaw. He trotted to his ledge and ate, but with eyes drawn on me. He swallowed, panted a bit, settled in to watch what was near him then got up to retrieve more of the supper he could find under neither rock nor sod.

"You like it? 'Cause if you do then get down here and take the rest. Don't make a libertine of me. Doesn't matter, crows'll be on it. They're no doubt hiding out here right now in the dark, watching every move. No? Not crow-hungry?"

I wanted him closer. I wanted him to take the bread from my hand — as one might, living up here without a single solitary pal in the world. I could tame him, if he ate from my hand. Get him inside. Have him sleep in the porch protected from all the scheming storms calculating out there right now over the Atlantic, laying winter battle plans for our dear old Highlands. I could cut out one of those little doggie doors in the bottom of my door and he could come and go as he liked after discovering how harmless at least one of the two-legs can be.

"Hey! Did I say you could go? Get the hell back down here and eat that! Don't come again, then, you snooty little rude red fox with your precious pelt and cattail tail. Here! Charlie!"

But he was gone to his high woods of night and in the morning was still gone when I flapped my arms and ran after Franklin, the crow gobbling the food I had left for the fox. But Franklin had a companion this morning, a missus — Francolene. Francolene often dug for slugs with Franklin in the lower built-up field. Franklin was the one with the wing that hung like a pedal with its cotter pin missing. But he could say hello. Who taught him, I don't know, but the bird knew man.

This is what I do know. I got a call from Mildred Molly, or Milly Molly they called her, a tough old woman in her eighties or so who had given birth to a dozen kids or more. I am holding back on her last name because it makes the woman too much of a fiction. But the name was Meaney. No — no man in the picture as far as I remember. But this Milly Molly Meaney fed, raised, and got those kids out into the world. She was the one calling my phone. I don't know why I answered. I felt I had to start making connection, I guess.

"I knew your mother in the hospital when she had ya," said the woman. "You're Miles, you're some kind of picture painter." She blew two big puffs then as if preparing to come to the point. I imagined trapped tobacco smoke exiting.

"I know they called you Kilometres. You were the one away who came home and won't talk to anyone. What's wrong wit cha? I heard them talk about ya at the store. You're a mouth organ player and were in a band overseas. The Tally Band. No, there's always some good in a person half-loony. I got these books here my brother got down in Colorado. I want ya ta take them. None of my gang ever read a solitary page and now they're dispersed all over hell's creation. So you come get them."

"Come get what?"

"The books, man, the books!"

Here we go — rampart breeched. I did know where she lived, though, over off of Meaney River. I hadn't been there since receiving crabapples for Halloween back in the seventies. Books, eh? Why do people think a musician must love music? That a painter must love paintings? I kept a journal, yes — well, then he must love reading! But how would she know I kept a journal when she thinks I'm a painter? " . . . I heard at the store": is how. I read all right, maybe a book a year. And my glasses were gone.

"All right," I told her.

Milly Molly Meaney's grown-in road turned left, turned right, then a hard, hard left that had me hauling on my handbrake because my floor brake was shot and I was going to go over the bank and into the river.

Decorated with wild flowers and crabapple trees, an old weathered house stood rooted in a riverbank. I got out into lupines that grew high as your ribcage. I shut my door, trapping some inside. My first real contact with the public.

There was a line of property spruce no doubt grown to act as windbreaks from the prevailing northeast. Branches were lopped off near the crowns, probably because they had obstructed a view. Her house topped an exposed bend of the Meaney River. Yes. I had been here, but outside the Halloween visit. I had come with Milly's son, Harrison. Yes, Harrison — the one to wear that Adidas outfit from primary up to high school. He was tall and slim and tried always to get out of work. We were hunting golf balls and had come as far as these fields. But Harrison also worked on the road with me as a fellow flagman. The boss asked him one day to shovel some rock and he folded like a carton, said he had a sore right neck and had to get to the hospital. I never saw him again.

At a rotted doorway, against the most solid post I could find, I tapped mud off my boots ever so lightly to announce my arrival. Cats had pissed in the vicinity. I looked atop a short fridge to see a fat druggy-eyed calico alongside an open tin and box of treats.

The old woman appeared from a blanket-draped door that looked like a wigwam entrance. She wore a housecoat and held a long-filtered cigarette like a movie star.

"Who are you?" she said in a smooth, high-pitched voice.

"You called me. I'm Miles, I'm here for the books."

"Miles. When did you get out? Miles, I haven't seen you since you were a kid. Boy did you ever change your life. Is it true you were all over the world? You got more gumption than most. You probably think I'm a joke. Well you listen, mister. I'm ninety-one and I live on my own. I see and I hear. I'm not someone who needs people around except for my daughter who brings groceries. I get up everyday and thank the Lord Jesus my Saviour I'm on my own, hear me?"

"I hear you."

"Books, eh? None of my gang ever read a single solitary page. But they were smart enough to get the hell out, though. Make a go of something some other place. Okay, I'll let ya have them but you promise me one thing."

"Promise you?"

"Yeah! Promise me!

"Okay. If I can."

"I want you to read them before I die."

45

"Thses here?"

On the table were eight weighty hardcovers with red spines.

"I want someone in this blessed community to take advantage of what knowledge is in thum. Our people's as good as the next. But you got to promise me, mister."

I looked at her. She didn't seem too spry. Eight books, eh? One year? I'll have to get those damn drugstore glasses but there aren't any drugstores here. A Sydney grocery trip, I guess. I looked at her and her heavy dark eye was on me, the slices or, wrinkles at her mouth working, a moustache with whiskers aimed right at me. I must have met with some approval.

"Good, then." She began her retreat. "The rest are in the old house at the top of the stairs."

"Rest?"

But she had gone in past her draped blanket where I heard a radio come on, a weather forecast. Three cats with long tails were at my legs. My eyes watered and burned and I wondered what leptospirosis I was catching. I carried the eight red spines through the lupines to the car, a load heavier than any wheel-barrow trip I had ever made.

Old house, eh? Top of the stairs? The old house was hidden by her newer one which I daresay could have taken the prize for "old" all on its own. In behind was this second one. I looked up at a bowed roofline here, as I eased past a puddle. I stepped over a really rotted doorsill and came inside to fetid air where a staircase confronted me. How many people were killed in here by one of her stay-at-home sons?

At the top of dangerous treads, feeling around with both feet for some security on the second floor, clutching a jamb, I did a double take. For in past a half-open door were the red-spined

books. Two stacks — me son! I eased the door open — two?
No, it was four stacks!

I counted fifty books, not a volume missing: "Five Feet of
Harvard Classics."

Five feet! Yalp! She'd better be prepared to tack on a
hundred years to the age she is now!

"Hello," I heard.

I turned.

"Hello?" I answered, waiting. It came from up above here
all right but had this raspy, sick quality to it. I entered the hall.
There? That room? Down the hall was a door. I didn't like at all
traversing up here. It came again.

"Hello."

"How are you?" I said.

"Hello."

What the hell? Who's living up here? Maybe it's one of her
children who never left. But why won't the he or she answer
better? Is there derangement?

I entered the room and saw a rocking chair. Newspaper was
scattered over the floor and there was an open window where
rain entered. Not a soul was in the room or the house.

"That's Franklin," said Milly Molly out to watch me load, out
in the air with her movie-star cigarette, her housecoat under a
flashy winter jacket. "The kids raised him and taught him how
to speak. They used firecrackers and a fish crate, bread, too.
But you get home, Miles. It's near dark, dear. I got to lock the
door. Good seeing ya again. Get some meat on them bones. You
should always be a little fat in case you get sick." I heard the
click of the lock.

"Hello," Franklin said. He had found me, over around the harbour here. He had come the very day after the books. He liked the power line.

Francolene flew up to him, settling alongside, getting her breast tight in against his but so much so that Franklin almost fell before he could get a wing out. She expressed discontent at his having flown off from where they searched the built-up field for slugs together. Franky-boy, it seemed, was her Complaints Department. Frankolene had sheen, was sleek, was young yet. But they kept me company, waiting for me to throw out bad cooking. Which is how clever these creatures are — for it was only a matter of time.

I closed out the night with a stomp of "A Part of the Sea".

> It's nice to be a part of the sea
> With the wind and sail in harmony
> It's nice to know as the cold wind blows
> That you're working for your family.

Blue Eyes

Iron-grey skies is what I remember of the place. It was cold and damp. Which make for the worse kind of winter for sniffles and cheap umbrellas, for the suffering faces of bad marriages, for the hangovers, and the dastardly work of mean parents. Everyone was rushing, legs working quickly and silently. This was the street scene in Hiroshima near the business district where I don't know why I was, except that it had to do with some class I had to teach. Up ahead was a pedestrian jam of some sort and an umbrella nailed me in the face, an overcoat collar got in my mouth, and diaphanous headwear spilt a cleft of water down my neck. Japanese pressed and pressed at my body and for a split second my feet were off the ground as I moved in mass and flow. I got balance back, got soles and knees back, and my elbows pushed at the force. But I had to see what it was on the sidewalk that created this mass aversion. There it was, dead centre, gripping concrete. A huge greasy, meaty, sewery rat with four legs out like the bug that hits your glass. Paralyzed with fear the thing didn't know where to go.

It was an autumn, that time when the leaves shout from the wet mountains across the harbour that there's been no better year than this for tints. Every time, every time I lifted my head to see the tapestry of the moment ago it had vanished and a new one was fully woven. So you look away just so you could look again. Mystery was in every move you made and you asked, "Why is it that here I am of all places and what is this age my bones know?"

I called to the woods, "Can't play the fiddle tonight, Charlie me son. Piece of steel in my knuckle, puttin'" up the flue. Fiddling days might be done. Old man's journal might be my occupation now."

A breath of lonely autumn answered and I saw that that one beautiful sad maple I knew so well had gone early again. It always took the prize for the winning leaf of October. In the wheelbarrow, I set my rake, my half-ton crowbar, and my pick with the new yellow handle I'd found.

I dug for an hour at the road, almost quitting — quitting everything, my knuckle aching. I studied the knuckle then looked up. Charlie was on the bank.

"Oh, you're not the first to come back for the bread. All I ever learnt, that. That and the fiddle and the guitar. I know I had enough of this work stuff. Years go by. Plus, there's fifty books to read — and I might have to do that inside twelve months."

I kept my tone even. I wanted him relaxed and relax he went. They say all mammals play. He did, he rolled and chased his tail the way cats do. So not all work for you forest folk, either? There's my lesson. I climbed the hill but by the back way, across the built-up field and behind the house. I tossed him the homemade bread.

"Enough, you! That's half a loaf ya got down! You know how much time that takes to prepare? No, that's right, don't listen to me. Get what you can while you can."

He was coming closer. Of course my goal was to get him to eat from my hand, or within reach. He wouldn't come. I set a piece on the step and backed up inside. I left the door open and put a fresh pinch on the porch floor.

"No? Smart enough not to enter, eh?"

He was there every night then, on his ledge, on his fiddle seat. I played despite my knuckle. It took coaxing and lots of pinches of bread to get him down on the hard ground. He didn't come near the step again.

"Guess you'll never trust me. But can't say I blame ya after what you wood folk have been through with our kind. But you're here all the time, too, aren't you Charlie? You got a good thing going is why."

At the cupboard, I took down the jar of peanut butter and walked-out a dollop on a piece of bread. I tossed this from the step and then snapped on the porch light to watch. He was on hard ground, his head lowered, sniffing.

"That's it, salty, sweet. But have you got room left in that fox-pocket stomach? Try it, new experience I assure you."

With it in his jaws like a hen he clucked, studying my eye always.

"*Muckt, muckt, muckt,*" his fox tongue went, twisting every which way.

"Peanut butter, Charlie. Revolutionary."

It took a time to get it off the roof of his mouth and when he did, he turned for his dark trees.

I watched till I saw him no more and then switched off the light.

The moon shone a silver rectangle onto the plank floor of the living room. The fridge buzzed. All was so beautiful I didn't move one inch.

The phone rang. It was my brother Paddy telling me what I expected. My father had died and I was so soon climbing the hill, with a six-hundred-page journal in my arms.

Inside the cover he had written, "The beginning and end of it all."

I called to the forest at the hour between the dog and the wolf. I turned from the little moon above the sea, my old man's fiddle in one hand, the other stationed on the corner of the house. And there he was, on the best seat in the house.

"No bread, no cracker, no cookie tonight, fox. But a heart a little broke. Here then, cheese, expensive, take it all."

I left him to his meal but there was whining and I turned.

He was in the porch.

I bent and he brought a stockinged leg forward, studying me as you would a pirate lending his hand for your rescue from a stormy sea. I left the porch door open and the cheese inside. He came in, looked around, sat, didn't take the cheese, and left.

"Get the hell down here! I ain't climbing up that!"

It was old man Blaze Dickey, Tim's hermit father, Blue Blazes they called him because of the colour of his shaved beard when he was a young man. He was the player of a homemade mandolin and walked below the house every Tuesday morning at nine to get his groceries around the harbour. During Lent he'd walk all the way over to church in the evenings for the Stations of the Cross. That's when they started calling him, Holy Blue Blazes. He had something slim and heavy in a plastic grocery bag.

He climbed to the apple tree. "See your fox today?" he said.

"Not today, Blazes," I said.

"Sorry to hear about your old man. That's what I come to say. He was one of the good ones. On his last visit here he told me he never would have left had he known at least one of his sons would return. And to think that it would be you to come back, the globetrotting you did. Your old man needed to be around the Halifax hospitals, I guess. What do ya call him?"

"Who?"

"Your fox. My kids had a seagull once they raised from a hatched egg. It would follow them to school behind the bus. Webster they called him. He'd hang around the play-yard the whole day then fly back behind the bus on the return home. What became of him I'll never know. Out in the Atlantic somewhere. But you earn the trust of an animal and they won't leave you. They'll teach you."

Sammy the Trapper's daughter appeared at the road. At my bad turn she moved and old man Blue Blazes and me ran dry like turned-off faucets. We waved when she was below and both said, "Good day," like a pair of dummies.

Blue Blazes took from his bag a big bottle of rum. "Here," he said. "Givin 'er up. Take it, in your hand. Yes, your father. Him and me walked home from the war together, from Sydney. A romantic, that Kenny. He had that big family but was the most practical man I knew. We were in France. He drove an ambulance and dealt with awful things. Hope you never asked him about it. He liked rainbows. But we're all cobbled together, us. Claw of a bear, foot of a partridge, beak of a seagull — sewn up and made to walk, to run. Even fly. Only one thing makes sense."

"Hope?"

"Hope? Go home, me son! Hope's an old nine-iron and putter sitting in the bag you had when the course opened. Too cheap to give them away so they're there in your shed in their drooping bag all through your life, in the way the whole time. Reconcile. Reconciliation. Your father was nowhere beyond France but look at all he accomplished. He understood that all you have to do is get together a meal, keep yourself safe, cobble together a night."

Blue Blazes shuffled down onto the Cabot Trail and waved before he went out of sight. And I saw no more of Holy Blue

Blazes Dickey on Tuesday morning at nine. He died, too, the grim reaper jamming them all under his cloak.

I did see his temporary grave marker: "Blue Blazes" they had quoted. I saw the marker when I was visiting my own father's grave and my mother's, the two of them buried side by side.

Up near the road a woman in a Cabot High jacket and baseball cap was scrambling off a ride-on mower full of smoke. She waved a work glove to dissipate the smoke. She waved the glove in my direction.

"Smoke," she hollered.

I raised my hand halfway. My folks did see the ocean from here. Gulls spun in the sun.

I had one big solid glass of Blaze Dickey's copper rum before me. It was all there'd be, because I had poured the rest down the sink. A chainsaw, power tools — they were of little note in comparison with the caution taken with booze up on a lonesome hill. I closed out the night with a stomp at the eleven-dollar of "Blue Eyes".

> Blue eyes, oh blue eyes
> Come back to me
> I'm here in the fields
> Of the Clyburn Valley
> Where are those gold mines
> You said I would see?
> Blue eyes, oh blue eyes
> Come back home to me
> Oh, blue eyes, oh blue eyes
> Come back home to me.

Charlie the Fox

Winston the Weasel squeezed his head out of a drift when I was taking a leak. His eyes were rate pink, and the rest of him slid around like a little bag of snow. My father's words came back to me, "Get one of those in your house and that'll be the end of it!" The end of what, I always wondered. Of a peaceful life, no doubt, in your house. In any case I threw a boot at him only to lose my footing and go slap bang down on my back. Ice, neatly sheeted under snow where rain had spilled off the eave and branched out to form a hidden rink.

Holy dyin old Jesus, how many ribs are broke? Serves me right, I suppose, throwing a boot at a weasel.

I saw him then, disappear through soffit and into the house. That made me rise — no, it did not. I couldn't.

What rose was the deathbed scene: the priest leaning over.

"You're hanging on?" he said.

"Am I not supposed to?"

"What was the thing with you that broke you?"

"Me? My heart? Driveway, Father."

I clutch that frock and collar of his, that black shirt of good cotton. "Driveway, hear me! Drive! Way!"

Ah my. I rise to an elbow, take in a big chest of air, snack on snow from a mitt. Ribs, for sure. No laughing for six months.

That took care of winter. It was summer and I looked for Charlie. I laid my daily three-feet of road; that is, three on each side. When I looked at my progress from up at the house I could see no progress whatsoever.

I was calling for Charlie when from over the roof, in an unbothered sky, sails this lovely afternoon cloud on its daily work and following was an eagle whose talons gripped a fir crown, an architectural bit to remedy some need in his shore home of the white pine.

I rose from bushes where I remedied the rib injury of last winter. I will be kilt up here. A truck slowed below.

"Going around the harbour. Want anything?"

"No, Sammy. Not a thing."

I had no money and if I did I would be the one to do the buying. I didn't know why that guy kept checking in. He must have felt we were a part of some team over here on Smokey.

The crows Franklin and Francolene sat on their electricity wire. She pressed in on him, seemed only content when his breast beat in conjunction with hers. He took steps to gain breathing space. "Doll, I know love is love but you're gonna knock me off here!" He sidled in more electricity-wire steps. She sidled too, squawking at this indignation. He drew back from her caws, fell, scrambled to catch his wings, swooped.

Life had been long. It also arrived here in a minute. I knew no more than I did as a boy as to what was going on. Summer was gone here, and my driveway tracks were up to the apple tree, halfway to their goal. Beside me was my wheelbarrow with its neat pack of pick, shovel and rake. Beside that was my fish tub, trowel, and the rubber gloves I used to mix the concrete batter. I remember asking at the hardware store how much water, how much aggregate, how much cement goes into a batch. I never got a straight answer. You get to feel what is right, as far as amounts go, as you do when making bread.

I drifted off in warm autumn grass, waking to quick rain. The tools could stay where they were.

In the house I was stirring up coals when the phone rang. It was the university-college. "We'd like you in for a little reasoning behind your course. There are songs here, personal songs. Yes, our Department of Folklore did suggest it in the Meeting of Heads. Yes, yes, a touristic flavour. But we're just not sure. Thing is, they're a bit on the folksy side."

They would put me up in their residence for a couple days.

The Rocket took me to town, the transmission doing fine after I got up over Smokey. The songs were chopped. The course was too, no doubt. I could keep the cheques. "We'll look at another course, if you care to put one together. But in the rational manner." I'll rational manner ya! Yalp, I'm putting together another course. No doubt.

Driving back I realized it was late October. A blackening sky gathered itself and I lowered the window because a warm storm was hitting and all that nostalgia of a couple hundred years of goodness that you once new but could never express flooded my mind. But by the time I got over Kelly's Mountain, my mind froze; the temperature had dropped fifteen degrees and the heavens were blowing the hell out of cloud-laced sky north. Every tint of grey fought to become a Mars black. And all tunneled way off to a black pit with tiny Smokey Mountain its protractor point — exactly where I was bound.

My Ford GT, the Rocket, aimed her scratched hood and wriggled her paintbrushed rear through lower blasts of road wind, road rain, road fog. Raked piles of woodland leaves broke to scream in Halloween horrors across a country road. My wipers washed; my poor dear muffler growled back there at a darkening night whose wind growled rate back: "Pipe down, you! The show's up here!"

I came to a stop, sat still in my car to face the Englishtown Ferry stationed on the far side, the Down North side; a black strait of irate chop boiled between us. A late night quality suddenly arrived as I pushed fingers in at the back of my neck, all this road maneuvering in a charging wind, in sailing rain knotting things up. But those guys don't see me over here, those ferry guys! They're probably drunk and passed out!

I flipped on the high beams after reading a good government sign: "Ferry Operators See You! Do Not Flip On Your High Beams!" You see me, eh? Now you do! When I did flip on the high beams I saw life, near life, storm life.

I opened the door to morbid rain and the life I saw was no shifting jellyfish blob blown up on the slip but a puffin, a deeply-soaked Atlantic puffin, the magic bird.

I had always seen these birds depicted on entrepreneurial road signs. They were the brightly painted woodcarvings in Cabot Trail gift shops. Restaurants and motor inns named their establishments after this bird of the high Atlantic shore, with its tropical beak. The bird had always been in my world yet I didn't know him from a hole in the wall. I had never seen one.

This one was storm-broke, stuck in his journey, worn out from the harsh play of an all-out hurricane that lands him and me smack dab on a black ferry asphalt with no power to go on. "Yes, true. I feel like you." Could I get him home to safe haven? I have to take care of something before all this is over. How about it, Puffy? Night of rest? What do you say to a night of rest where it's dry and no one wants anything from you, which we're lucky to get even for one night, this life. You'll be free to go come morning. That is a victory immeasurable.

She, he — I couldn't say which but it shot under my car when I went for it. And on my knees, my palms, my poor cheek on a soaked ferry ramp smeared with brake fluid and motor oil and gum and phlegm I said, "Come here, you little bastard! The boat's comin'!" She was near the rear axle, between the tires, waiting in her curling-rock silhouette. I entered the Rocket, reversed it ever so slightly to have there come the teeniest of bumps. Ut oh.

Out I got as the wild wind grabbed my door like a fed-up bouncer. Under I got and all was as feared. I lifted the little life left and set all in ornamental grass bordering on the higher ramp east, where there was coverage from a wild night, and maybe a kind sun to rise on you.

The ferry lowered her black soaking boarding fin and I drove on. The ticket collector came to my window. "You're out tonight." It was a statement, a question — you could do what you want with it.

"A fact," I said, easing up the window, installing the two booklet tickets left in the molding of the upholstery above.

When the ferry let me off on the Down North side I drove up the ramp, swung around the cable house, and boarded again. The ticket man had his hands in mid-chest pockets, an oil-barrel of a fellow. I rolled down my window to rain on my face. He asked nothing but leaned forward.

"Forgot something!" I hollered into the wind.

"People forget things here all the time!"

"Do I have to pay to get on again?"

He shook his head left then right and I waited for what this meant. He might have been exercising his neck. He entered his very bright cabin as me and the Rocket waited in the gales on a sloshed and bucking deck.

What I forgot was to bury the creature, to dig, to claw wet earth with my fingers, set him inside, pat down black soil with gravelly palms and a hurt knuckle. All waking, all walking, crawling and inching deserve some respect, where possible.

I drove up off the ramp and saw in my rear-view the ticket collector. He had come to watch me exit his storm-washed decks. Or, to see what I was up to. I saw he was a bigger man than I had him pegged as, but maybe with pride he swelled like the Japanese blowfish. I am sure he had his eye on my vehicle as he policed the night world of his black beat.

I clutched at sharp grass, my hands discovering only well-rooted blades. I went through the whole patch. Nothing. I drove up the road to turn, to kill time, to make my story less suspicious for the ferryman. When I signalled for the tiny dark, wet post office of Englishtown — where no town exists — in my signal flashes I saw a red fox trot with the puffin in its mouth.

On the ferry, the collector in good government gear said, "You're not sure what ya want to do tonight!"

"To get home is what!"

"That way, then!" He pointed Down North where all was as black as the lower reaches of an abandoned Brazilian goldmine. "There's where you live, my son!" he said.

Jez, the man knows where I live. You want to get discovered? Come to the sticks. We think we go unnoticed, we do not. And tonight I really got myself written up in the annals. I heard in my inner ear their big chat by the hot ferry boiler: "Pass the cup, then I says to him — that's where *you* live, bai! Yes, that's right — him! He's the one! That Down North musician fellow who was all the hell over hell's creation and had that time overseas. All that to come home with no more sense than a bedbug. Night like this — out! Pass the bottle!"

From the ferry on down the North Shore the trees used every inch of their root not to be pulled from the frame of the world. The image of that fox going with the puffin in its mouth brought Charlie to mind. Charlie? Damn, I forgot you! What have I done! Poor, poor Charlie. We had an agreement, the two of us — I played the fiddle between the hour of the dog and the wolf; he trotted off the mountain for his morsel. On this wild night and two previous I had forsaken him with my trip into town. And all for naught, they hated the course — damn, you university-college! There with commitment, Charlie had been, every night for weeks and weeks. How could I have at least forgotten to leave something for him? That animal was teaching me, all right, to get a little food, have a little peace of mind, and all would fall into place. But no. I head off without the least regard.

I motored up my hill, tires ripping recent track work, spoiling raked gravel and store-bought sod. Mud flew, stone flew from a concrete undermined by rain. I was spinning, slipping, not making progress. I yanked my wheel to the right, to the left, gunned it, rocked the front wheels when it was my headlights at last that seemed to pull me up out of it all like a space shuttle leaving orbit. I got to level ground and got out. Charging rain ran past the illumination of my backdoor light.

I was on the step: "Charlie!"

My groceries were in the car, the house door slung flamboyantly open, a long door-curtain trailing like the gown of a spoilt virgin. I played my fiddle, "The Smokey Jig", a tune of old flair as the instrument's aged wood got wetted alongside a black night forest.

I shone a flashlight with good battery to see what I could but rain only poured there like it was stuff from the world's first storm. I extinguished the light and studied all from the back step below the backdoor light where currents ran branded from heaven. My hair was pasted to a knotted forehead, a forehead wearing too many of life's long concerns. That fox had eaten from my hand. Had come to my music. I could have got him inside. Made him a pet. The groceries — in the car? Anything there for him? Cheese, but buried.

I kicked my toe in the greasy bank, dug in my hand, clutched and climbed to his ledge and there, in the backdoor light, gleaming like gold crying, were my father's glasses.

I put down the pen and looked at the paper, I closed out with "Charlie the Fox".

> *For years and years*
> *I combed the land*
> *Up hill and down valley*
> *For my father's golden glasses*
> *I lost up on Cape Smokey*
> *Round the harbour in the old house*
> *In the cold room that was mine*
> *In against the china cabinet*
> *I found them down behind.*

A Cape Breton Connection

Two bald eagles had reached maturity. After much extending of their long wings, they parted from the pine for the world of flight. I was brushing my teeth at dawn on the deck east when I heard a squawk. There was martial brushing down over the bank; it was that same electricity that is in the air when a crime is going down. From the car-sized settlement, I saw two bodies drop, four wings, opening like plywood robbed by the wind.

Shadows flushed over green needles of spruce tops and ushes and whooshes marked the harbour air as these shadow-makers fell plumb into a life of air.

"Yesss!" said Tim. "Or should I use the local — Yalp! Which translates to I don't believe ya, me son!"

Like a pudding on an active clothes dryer, Tickety Tim Dickety waited by the woodstove in my purple chair. He was out of breath. His truck was in the paint shop so he had climbed the hill with his stick; his jowls were red, his front tooth blackened from a fall after a recent binge.

"A tree fell on me, Miles," he said, of the tooth. "I put up my hand and, bang-o. But Charlie? Is that right? I mean you didn't go and leave them there on his ledge? Because we do things like that."

"Are you out of your mind? I didn't leave these on no ledge! I looked around that ledge probably a thousand times. They were covered in grass and bits of that black mud from up on the flat by the Tree Ghost. They looked born of the earth theirself. Wherever they were, they were planning to stay a while."

"You figure he had them in his den? Or that he just dug them out of the mud and brought them? Maybe he kept them in his den till he could use them."

"I think he just found them in the woods and brought them down. He connected them with me — which is food. He saw me in them, too, remember, that first day."

"I'd call the paper in Sydney. This is a Personal Interest story."

I looked at him here and he looked at me. My look said, 'How much do you know me or, of me? Personal Interest . . . Jesus.' His look said, 'Did I mess up again? I'm just talking, Miles.'

"But foxes are attracted to golf balls," said Tim. "They steal them off the fairway with the ball in play. I seen that. They have nests in the woods that they fill with golf balls. Came across one of those, too. Smells good in here. You got the old bread going? Someone told me — was it you? — about treasure-troves the crows have. And fish like gold; don't forget. Whoever stumbled upon that got us our first trout."

"You want bread?"

"Anything to go wit it? Or are ya still on that Sanskrit diet?"

"The *what* diet?

"All that toll-food and bean curd — I thought they were saying *toad-food*. You know, what they had you eatin' over there."

"Do you want peanut butter?"

"Slap her tagether."

"I baked a second loaf that I'm sticking on the ledge."

"Don't cut into the second."

I looked up. His hands were behind his head and he was studying the cathedral ceiling and talking to a point of missing crack-fill. "You put that up on the ledge and he continues — not to show, watch how old Franklin will have a good old hoe into that loaf quick enough."

"I'm watching for him, and for her."

"Who? The woman crow? Frankolene?" he said. I was coming with milk for his tea. "That's a good idea, though, a loaf." He was staring at me now, talkative because someone was waiting on him. "Those gold-rim spectacles look the clear thing on you, Miles. Your face is straight from the twenties."

"I see at least."

"It's good to see."

"There's all that reading I have to do."

"Drugstore glasses, no good?"

"Not like prescrips. Lost the drugstore's."

"Well, don't lose these again. Get a rope for thum."

"Rope?"

But he was staring at the fire and lost to any previous topic.

He transferred himself onto the fish crate that held the wood poker. He nudged himself nearer the fire and stretched a halting palm toward it, appearing a smaller man suddenly. His girth disappeared, the way he sat. His shoulders narrowed and he seemed hardly the man to handle the heavy work of lobster traps. Yes, bad luck had settled on the man's frame.

"You're losing weight, Tim."

"I'll soon be like you. I come here for rest," he said. "You got a peace up here you may not even know about. It always feels like the power's out. That's good. Another world's down there, me son. Power's on down there, me son, she's full force."

"A flat world is down there too."

"A flat world that gets harder and harder to step back down on ta." Sights out the window east occupied him, gulls and breakers most likely. The man's eyebrows needed trimming.

"What's going on, Tim?" I said, setting him up with a teaspoon.

"What's not goin' on? Ah, I told ya. The girlfriend."

"You called her that before. She's your wife. You even got the wedding band."

He touched the band.

"I downgraded her. Or, upgraded her. Or she upgraded me."

He studied the driveway and I knew what was coming.

"When ya ever gonna finish that?"

"Are you divorced, Tim?" I looked at him here but he kept his eyes off me.

"Divorced? Nice luxury! Who can afford that? Yes, divorced I am — taking winter trips to Las Vegas, too, to one of those club meds on the beach. She wants her status as girlfriend. Fine by me, I said. It's some kind of Facebook thing. She won't even friend me, though."

"Friend me?"

I placed the buttered toast, the jar of peanut butter, and hot tea in a pot beside him. He received this as the played-out do — not seeing what the other has done; looking ahead like the kid who can't tie his shoe, waiting past word for his mother to do it.

"Thank you," he said.

"What's the trouble, Tim, really?"

"Really? Just the damage people do, to each other. It ain't fit. She loves me, she says, when I'm there. When she's off on her own she has single thoughts, she says. I put two and two together. She's doin' it with this here landlord's son, a young Philip guy who's out at all the bars all the time and this is all just new experiences, for him. We got kids. She's with him, in a spot I borrow money to pay for. Ah bai, that old Minglewood song, all right — I'm gonna take a freight train from the station, all right, but west! And I ain't never coming back! Funerals, maybe. See you, maybe. No Miles, I didn't make much of a go."

"Go?"

"Of life. Life, man! She says she's moving in with this fella to Dad's old place. Down here."

His fingers were knitted over his knee and his skin grey and thin like the fog. I wasn't sure if he knew where he was. In my purple chair he looked to be a man of a hundred and five. He wore his Cabot High jacket, of thirty years back, the one that woman at the graveyard had on. Anyone who wears those have either surrendered or never started. I remembered the day he took the jacket out of the plastic. "What the hell's this?" he had said. "Oh yeah, jump rate on the bandwagon like everyone else! Get a high school jacket, oh yeah!"

"Miles?" he said to me.

"What?"

He was looking at me, all this was important to him.

"What, I said? Eat the bread, Tim, I prepared for ya."

"I said — I didn't make much of a go of it!"

He took a bite.

"Where'd this all happen, Tim? In town? That where you are now?"

"In town. Here. I'm all over, me son. She's moving in the old homestead with her boyfriend because I can't afford their apartment. That's Dad's place, bai. She even had him visiting when Dad was alive. Look out when they say — he's just a friend. I'm in the pop-up trailer across the road. I can't take any more of it so I'm bound for west is what I come to say. The kids need real raising, which translates into dough and rei from — me! They need better than her or me. I'm all mixed up, tell ya the truth and I don't know how it came to be. I was happy. I know people say that all the time — but I was! Last thing I do before heading her off to bed is make sure I got a bottle for the morning. Yalp, Fort Mac."

"Where's that, Tim?"

"Now, go home! Miles! Me son! Did they keep the whole world from ya over there? Fort Mac? Mac as in MacMurray? Out west, Miles. Alberta tar sands. Where all go. Where the road to catch up starts. Or, ends."

"You did no wrong, Tim. Bit of poor luck is all."

"Ya got the poor part right."

"You shouldn't have to go." I came near the fire, I could smell his boot heating up.

"There's another option?" he said, grimacing in the heat.

"First hand — ah, I don't know. You did nothing wrong."

"That's right and yet, wrong comes." He was speaking to the flames, past the glass.

"Tim? Tonight. Stay in the boathouse tonight. You need a break, man. Go to the shore. There's running water, a stove."

"Would you mind it, Miles?" He looked straight at me as if I was giving him the go-ahead after waiting years as a refugee to pass into a country of promise. Yes. Help I was giving Tim but also I was deferring his case, to the tides. I had no experience, no authority — how wrong we are here.

"Would I mind it?" I said. "Tim? No, I wouldn't mind it. We're here for each other, I hope so anyway. We'll carry you down a couple blankets and a lantern. There's stew. Fill up on that."

"This bread'll do. I kind of gave up eatin', a lot, I mean. What will I do down there?" What would he do? He knew. He carried a flask. "Can I take one of those books? I never read one, you know."

His fingers were knit around his gut, his nose red and pitted, his hair falling out but his tone carried just that bit of hope.

"Never read one?" I said. "What? One of the red-spines?"

"A book! Maybe that's what's wrong with me."

"There's nothing's wrong with you, Tim. Nothing that ain't wrong with the rest of us."

He shook his head; a painful memory plagued him, I would guess. He stood to get away from the thought, what it was that bothered him. He went to the bookshelf.

"I'm gonna choose one."

"Choose one, choose a book to read."

"Look at the red ones, will ya? They the set old Milly Molly gave ya? I told that old dear about you over here reading."

"*You* did!"

"I saw her at the Freshmart one day, poor old thing in the aisle. Someone had to speak to her. But what did she think? You had a few years in pris . . . I never did, ya know, read one."

"No crime in that."

"Only punishment — this good? *Crime and Punishment?*"

"A landlady gets halved with an axe."

"Good for her because I couldn't finish that in ten years time."

I came to the case, I selected one for him.

"Here. *Trees of Nova Scotia*. Ninety-one pages." I also gave him *The Wanton Troopers* by Alden Nowlan. He passed this back but kept *The Trees*.

We laid out a bed of fish netting as level as possible. The lantern burned its pine-scented oil to brighten the shack walls. We hauled a mattress from the loft. I laid the two woolen blankets atop of it.

"Always good to sleep in army blankets," said Tim. "Makes you feel what the soldiers felt, but without the gettin' shot." He was fussy, wanted to forgo the mattress and bed down on the netting. "I'm too worn out for a mattress, Miles." I could almost catch the logic but there seemed more of a resentment toward the mattress.

"The toilet bowl works," I said. "The pipe runs out into a plastic bait-tub. Out there in the loose gravel, back up from water's edge."

"That old stove work?"

"Nah, the other one does, though. But that one's the real old-timer stove, a great bread-baker, she came out of the old house. I got a key to the big place on the hill hidden down under the grates there — on the cold side, that I would come and get all those times I was away. If I ever disappear you know where to find it. Make sure you grab my journals from the house. Sorry, Tim. It's just I don't sleep up at the house or else you'd be up there with me."

"What're you sorry for! Miles? Everyone knows Miles MacPherson don't sleep. You're like a squirrel in the attic. They see your light on over here from the Woody Shore every night. They hear either your chainsaw or that little guitar with all the drawings on it or your fiddle. Who's not got demons, Miles? What's done is what's done and we just got to live with the contradictions, you and me and everyone else. Miles?"

"Yes?"

"This is great down here. Miles?"

"Yes, Tim, yes — what is it?"

"My jacket'll be my pillow and what man doesn't like to sleep like the cowboys? Best place in the world for someone who needs a solitary look at things, seashore. Oops, I upset your pencil cup." A pencil rolled on the floor. I grabbed it.

"That's right. You forget about her and about all your troubles."

"She ain't in the picture. Her and me live in different worlds. I'm all right, Miles. And I'll keep a good eye out for that Charlie of yours. I wouldn't mind catching a glimpse, just once of that fella."

"He is real."

"I know he's real. But listen to the racket of those crows, will ya? Is that what that is? And here it is, night! Was there ever as crazy a community than the crow community? What did you call them when they're together — murder, was it?"

Tim was giddy, heavily possessed of the hyper part of that mania he was prone to. But he smiled in it, calm as a waking kitten suddenly, raising his palms to me as if to show he had no gun.

I nodded, pretended I understood. "Must be Franklin and Francolene," I said.

"Those two?" he said. "You told me about them."

"She's a bull of a partner. Every time I see her she's pressing herself in on him."

"Go on?"

"Hard old love, Tim."

I looked at him. "Franklin was a loner for the longest time."

"He the hello bird? Loner might be the way to go."

"A bent wing tells you who he is."

"Does he still say hello?"

"All the time."

"Big hello?"

"Big enough. Tim? You get to sleep. Read your book." He was studying the crossbeam, the long frolicking shadow the lantern caused it to throw.

"Tim?"

"Right here, chief."

"I always had a good feeling about you." He wouldn't look at me. "It's all work, Tim. And it'll all work out, too. Life is just lots of little systems to manage. Come to the window here. Above, see there? The big pine?" We looked out a black window at a black pine on the steep bank in the night, stars poking way up past it.

"Where?" he said.

"That big clump, half driftwood, half bough. That's the eagle's nest."

"Go on?"

His eyes were big and were near me and I saw how the sparkle had gone, how they were dry like a contagious man's.

"An eagle flew crowns of fir down off the mountain to build it."

"Go on?"

"Lime Rickey green. There was this fragrance falling as his talons came over the gable-end, a wind rushing through like lungs blowing out candles."

"Ain't that something."

"I'll be down first thing with breakfast. You have the lantern. Read."

"I'll start that as soon as you leave . . . Miles?"

"You got to tell me — what is it?"

"I know you lived a hell, Miles.."

"The thing is what's before us, Tim."

"I know", he said. "I know."

He nodded. He stood in the doorway, book in hand, over his shoulder those shadows wavering and sniggering like bad people at a bad party.

I looked back when I was on the path and there he was, encouraging me, there in the doorway, hardly a man fit for sleep.

I climbed with the aid of the strong old bristly fishing rope that I had tied to an abandoned light pole up on the highway. It's a hellishly steep bank and that old car waited halfway up. I eased my gold glasses up the bridge of my nose, holding taut the prickly rope. My balance was good, hearing keen, nose keen. I felt strong in the way you do when in a dream you find yourself back in youth and all that aging was lie upon lie. The gold spectacles did it. I had them back on and the close world was returned to me. Decisions would be fine, now. And all else. That was the sense.

I walked the high dry road and heard my steps offset by a rumble of breakers down on the far side the Gut. I hollered loud as I could:

"Timmmm!"

"Right here, champ, down on the beach."

"Can you hear me, Tim!"

"All I do is hear you! What do you want, Miles?"

"For you to get ta bed! Timmmm!"

I listened as the echo rounded the harbour and back like a local petition.

"Get to bed!" I said.

"It's to bed I'm gettin'," he said.

And, *It's to bed I'm gettin'* dies out in the night air. And, *It's to bed I'm getting* dies out in the night air on any night. There were no crows. No breeze for the trees. Only a crescent moon pushing through crowns and a black cloud series closing over the Big Dipper. It was not all that cold. Tim would be A-Okay down in the tides.

Winded, I stood on my back step. The only light on was that of the bedroom nook east. How lonesome a home this is. Way up in the trees. But only as lonesome as are all homes, in one way or another. In the morning I will get that man up here away from the oily currents and have him stay with me till he gets back on his feet. That's my new project — to forget myself for a while, help someone out. Tim needs to end that Fort Mac talk. Even the title of that place frightens me. I've lived in places like that. They don't do for a man like Tim. I saw his anxiety. Things have gone awry for poor old Tim for a long time. The apple tree incident sparked it, the scrape in that paint job he was so proud of. Responsibility there was mine. I put the road in. I put this house up. What the hell is wrong with me anyway? Spending a life building a driveway?

I came back down that driveway, gravel underfoot, cool air on my forearms. Toil was the sense, here at the apple tree and I remembered how that stranger had stopped his truck out on the Cabot Trail that one hot evening. He had grown-out hair, was slouched but attentive and was perhaps not so far off from my age. He studied my work through mirrored sunglasses, a clam-flat sunset in each lens.

He said, "Think that'll work?"

This was the beginning of the driveway and on that evening I did not think it would work. I was bent with my pick. The words seemed the man's first speech of the day, the aching quality were in them. He had obviously had dreams of his own but it was getting late for them. In fact, chances were he would not now ever get to what he wished. I struck bedrock and shivers ran the course of my arms. And, there he was still, stationed out there, truck running on the Cabot Trail.

"We can only see," I said, not turning, not giving him me.

"We can only see," he parroted, twisting his head largely, not quite driving off but hands turning his wheel slightly — another half-moment, he was taking, to confirm these, the hard aims of man. Yes. Stepping around futility and puddles was best, after working it through your mind. The man felt for his gas pedal then, sent gas to his engine's chambers as rubber and rim burned slowly for the Salt Lake and the sunset, of a warmed Clam Flats.

I climbed to Charlie's ledge. I stood to see the white wash of the black ocean breakers, how all entered this side of the Gut. I touched my boot toe to the loaf of bread; heavy dew was on the crust. Franklin and bride Frankolene will get their share.

"Tim!" I hollered. But nothing came back, nothing but bleak tides lapping. Ah, leave him be, I said. Keep being tough, the way you do. It's the only way.

Timothy Thomas Dickey, age forty-nine, called it quits that night and like little else to come before, it ripped the heart out of a community one thousand strong. He had taken the fishing rope from the bank and with it hanged himself.

I cut him down. I tied slack around his waist, sawed my knife through the noose, then lowered him onto the floor.

You're not supposed to touch a body. I was not going to let him hang in his weight another second.

A blinding sun entered the window east during this. It no doubt would have done him good to see it. And yet, what do I know of what another sees?

The business of concluding a life of forty-nine years was over in days, the community proving itself strong and swift. The church forbade his inclusion in the graveyard, in this day, in this age. And the State could press no charges. His cousins had him cremated and a little ceremony took place locally. I asked for a little of the ashes and snuck some into the churchyard near a birch where I set a tiny stone I carved him, just under the ground him and stone went, right by some roots. I carried the rest up the mountain and tossed all over the look-off.

I climbed onto Charlie's ledge on the way down, found the loaf picked to pieces. I took what was left and flung it over the bank when out of the trees the two scavengers flew for it, taking all they could, in safety.

I closed out the night on the little guitar, with a stomp of "A Cape Breton Connection".

> As the waves crash over the ocean
> As the Highlands they fill with snow
> Got an island in my heart
> So haunting and stark
> And it plagues me wherever I go.

Rain Oh Rain

When the sun would set and the danger of collapse lessened I would enter the Saudi desert. Call to prayer came but I could hear my shoes crunch sand. I followed a fox till it disappeared in a hole. I was looking in the hole when a snake leapt from the sand and bit my forearm. It struck above the musical cleft scar left from a jellyfish off the coast of Brazil. I felt woozy but got back. I woke on the kitchen floor, the red puncture holes looking like the sharpening of musical notes. And above the musical cleft scar, if you read music, I wore the key of D.

My mother was dying. With clarity of voice she lay on a hospital bed. She asked me about the mark on my arm. She thought it was a tattoo. I asked her why she had let me go alone up the mountain that night as a boy.

"You, Miles? You needed a little extra."

I was past the Cradle, on the look-off where the wind caught Tim's ashes. When my hand came back, a finger caught the sharp, dried detailing of his stick. I sucked blood. This knuckle had the piece of steel. Why do we hurt what's been hurt? And it's right beside this other scar from the day I grabbed the hatchet blade. That was over there. Above the scree. One the mountain above the old house.

I had come home from school and set my books on the table.

Mom was baking bread, always baking bread.

"I'm going up the mountain," I said.

She looked at me, her eyes black like a raven in the rain.

"For the night," I said.

She nodded her head. "Go ahead."

I walked into my room, the northwest corner of the house, the Cold Room, I had named it. I sat on my cot and turned for the window, *Go ahead.* I'm not twelve and I get to, *Go ahead.*

I set an elbow below the sheer and looked out at Allan, Archie, Murray, Tommy, Larry, Reid, Greg, Bradley, Jimmy, Timmy, Wanda, Alice, Lisa, Marty, Sandy, Sylvia, and April. My siblings brought their friends here. Our big family was the collector lanes on highway. The kids played German ball, flew garbage-bag kites, ran with switches and rims, turned bicycles upside down to run the pedals with their hands. Why couldn't I be that — them? Enjoying this time as another happy-go-lucky, as these sisters did, these brothers, these neighbours. My elder siblings worked Alberta jobs, read books at colleges, lived on streets called Charlotte and Dorchester in Sydney. Where's Sydney? What is Sydney? I rolled up a cowboy and Indian sleeping bag, a trade made with Michael Jackson who had just entered the field, a rifle in a garbage bag, one more item for trade.

A hatchet was in the china cabinet. Where would matches be? In the kitchen I slapped peanut butter on a slab of baloney set on homemade bread. Yeast worked where my mother had a pail of dough covered in a towel by the stove. She worked her dough at midnight and you'd hear the legs of the table strain. Dough spikes were in every towel you dried off with. "There's an orange there," she said. I couldn't even see her. I couldn't see the woman who condemned me to a night in the woods. She hung clothes, at the porch window, her clothesline going *squeak, squeak– clip, clip — squeak, squeak.*

With the kitchen door open, that long steel coil above, ready to bring all rushing shut, I waited. I smelled rabbit fur in the porch, gun oil and iron filings from the grinder.

"Goodbye, Mom."

In my jean jacket, I walked to the road to discover all the others had disappeared. Wind touched my face. It was one of those old autumn winds that send you back a thousand years and give meaning in every step you take. The kids were in the trees, I saw at last, in the long grass, in the valleys of the roof where autumn leaves sailed gaily.

I crossed the double white line of the Cabot Trail.

Like ancients in their moaning knocking dance, giant poplars were above the ditch of these foreign properties across the road. Their leaves were upset about choral arrangements and late flowers. I didn't look back for my siblings. I heard their scuffs on roof asphalt.

At the bank which falls off for the Clam Flats I dug the toe of my sneaker in loose soil and climbed the bank like a ladder. My hand was on young fir with sharp needles then and I was in a steep forest next where cold, prominent, haughty trees stood sheer like winter rain. I ducked, I crept. Up fast I went in rising terrain, grabbing young trees to gain more and more elevation, my mother-cut hair allowing drafts in at the back of my neck. She had washed these pants I had on in her wringer washer so they were tight and good for a year. I don't know whose jacket I wore. It was woodsy.

I came upon scree that had red oak pushing through. Scree's the expansive slanting field of tumbled rock from the ice age. It's filled with cracks and holes and feels like you are jumping from car to car. I was halfway up when in a crack under my leg I saw a pair of eyes. My heart took one big beat and I skedaddled off that scree as quick as I could.

I had come to a cliff, where trees met stone that climbed much higher than them. I caught hold of a sapling that never quite got the promised sun and climbed. In two minutes I felt I should get down from there because a clean death-wind was in my face. My rolled sleeping bag caught a branch and I turned ever so gently to free it. This was the first of keeping your head cool.

I dragged myself onto a ledge, and one that overlooked my world. I saw Smokey, the great pink prow above a wide sea east where birds dipped for water or worked for height. I saw the harbour where my brothers were in the rowboat heading for the hermit of the Clam Flats. Village roofs came into sight and what I knew was their isolation.

Daylight's shift was ending. The sky west became the hue of lobster shells tossed in the garden. There was a drop and I looked above — sap? Sap doesn't drop. Clouds had amassed. They boiled above Smokey. I checked my sleeping bag. Two cowboys had suffered a tear, an Indian was shredded. Rain was on the sea. I took out my hatchet and I started a lean-to.

A lean-to is a half roof of light trees for your person to crawl into during a night in a forest. You have two upright poles and a lateral crossbar. Upon this you lean saplings at forty-five degrees, using joints of lopped off branches to establish structural support. You cover all in with boughs you weave in place and then you lay out soft branches for your bed. Your sleeping bag goes on this and you pray the gales are not severe, the cold, the wet, not inhumane.

I lay to test it. But sunlight hit the cliff and so I went and sat in its rays, my shoulders warming through my jean jacket.

But icy wind rushed from scree, a wind of winter that hid in the cracks there and lived here year-round. The smell of rain was in the spruce and pine. I drew up my collar. I had no whisker but knew in an instant that all the frosty seasons hid not only in the scree up here but in the plants and the soil. It merely waited for the coming of any given night.

I got in my lean-to and ate my sandwich. I peeled the rock-hard orange but then got up to spit the seeds over the cliff. They fell with no sound way down there onto a tree branch, between a rock, in a dark soil where they would never spring to life.

The sleeping bag was over my shoulders. I was on the ledge. The autumn woodland descended to an inky harbour. The boys were returning from the hermit's. Across the way, mountain tapestry there rose to more scree — three patches before passing up for a blackening sky, where trees shoot free of the ridge, to stand double and even triple the size of their black counterparts.

I saw the double-white line of the village road, the signs in miles. But no car, no tire, no Smokey traffic even, just me up here with a fearful silence that settled in my throat. I shifted weight and saw our house where a sister was getting back in off the roof by way of her upstairs window. I wondered if all of us were poets.

It does not darken first in the east but all over in a sky remote like ours. Black mountains brood equally when bloodied and beat. How many hours is a night? I was in my sleeping bag, my clothes on, my collar covering my ears. My hatchet was over my chest; a hatchet is a heavy icy tool. Balsam was between my fingers; it had worked itself into my mouth. I looked — my eagle eye noted seven-past-seven on the Timex I found on the beach. I heard the ticks. Sevens are good numbers and also terrible ones — they show how early it is, how long it is to go. Patter came in the needles above. It wasn't serious. There, there, you good forest, get some tasty rain.

Mom? Does she realize she has her child up here at seven after seven? A gum-smacker, she smacks now as she turns for the black-and-white TV at the warm oil stove below her drying rack, in apron she stands, flat shoes, where she works the grates. She looks through a crowded living room, scans for the one missing. A raft of kids sit on an industrial furnace grate. And above their Dad warms his feet on a square foot of its metal. He is in his wood chair under the bare hundred-watt bulb, a book on his lap, a mechanical study, a history — open at that same page from the last two nights, his famous golden glasses, awry over his shut eyes. A pile of books jammed in behind his chair, their covers ripped off, margins marked up with pens held in forceful grip; picture, illustration, artwork — all gone to school projects. But above, the wall adjacent the furnace, was the art — the descending line of musical instruments hung on nails that found studs, descending like a photo of seven young sons arranged by age: the arch-top with f-holes, the cat-gut classical, the banjo, the mandolin, the old violin, the ukulele, a squeezebox.

The rain did not get to me. It did not penetrate leaves and boughs. And it could be the case that you don't get ever wet in the woods. The leaf stops water from rushing below, the needle clutches at big drops. A tree is tall. A forest has many. You were snug and even happy to hear rain.

I wish I could say how untrue this was. For all that falls in a forest north makes straight for you, in your cowboy and Indian sleeping bag. I moved my hand to check my watch and in doing so sliced it on the hatchet. I sucked blood.

Oh, I was getting it good under the weeping lean-to. The open side actually brought relief. Was this why the structure was left open? To vacate, when rain came? Or the bear? I dug in. I closed my eyes and opened only to realize there was no difference. Light had ended so decisively that I felt dizzy. This proud eagle eye to find any lost ball on any hole at the golf course was nothing in a world lost of rods and cones.

The thing about the woods at night is that it is alive. Romps, thumps, bumps, crashes, scurries, and run-downs abound. I was an eyeball of wakefulness, clutching my hatchet, curling my knees, trying not to hear scratch, scratch, thump . . . prance, pounce, click, squeak. And? Thud . . . And? . . . No, not the pulling of a tree? What pulls a tree, at night? What lets it go with this, swoosh? Was that a growl?

God in Heaven the wondrous things I will do with my life, everyday till the end, you get me out of this. I cannot leave. I will fall off a cliff. I felt for my watch but in a black so complete I didn't know which wrist I touched. Wind began. Wind? Good, wind. Blow, blow, blow wind, and drive it all away. These animals, their activity. But will it? A storm will. A storm will drive them away.

Rain struck properly, wind struck properly. I was soaked and saved but tuck-in time was here.

There'd been no night not slept in my experience. I knew waiting, but never a night of it. And then I saw through the trees the red light of the Gut; it had been there all along. I knew this light. I saw it from the porch at night. So it would be my ally. And that? That slight tint in a sky east. Yes, black grew to grey.

I rose, I got on the peak, my soaked sleeping bag draped over me. I sucked dry blood. This was dawn. God, thank you and you have my promise. I will never do anything like this again. I have learned and have been ruined for stepping beyond the safe and the normal.

Trees leaked, the rain was over. I took a breath and could almost fill up my belly on the smell of pine in the rain.

I lowered myself over the cliff, looking back at my lean-to, thinking of what another would think to come across it. But I slipped, and somehow got back on the ledge — Jesus! After getting through a night like that — nice way to go! I rolled up my cuffs, set my sleeping bag on my back better, shoved my hatchet through my belt.

I was on the mountain flats, making good time over good ground. Copper needles were underfoot and I paid only cursory attention to animal prints left in the muck by the Mill Brook . . . Mill Brook? Yes — this meets the Cabot Trail!

Back at the house my mother was in the kitchen.

"How was your night in the woods?"

"Good," I said.

"Wash your face then, and get to school."

I began the guitar in the Cold Room. I asked my father right after that if I could try the guitar. He took it from the nail. I never knew this as being anything other than wall art, never knew that if you touched a string at an interval, the disturbed air changed your mood. We had no record player. The world was that old-man Cape Breton fiddle music, those loitering high-diddley-hoes in a little village you were never leaving because there was no money and what the hell was out there anyway? I had written a poem in the Cold Room after the journey up the mountain. I put it to chords my father had dug into the china cabinet frame with a hunting knife. I sang "Rain Oh Rain".

> *It rained on the day that you left*
> *Ruining your lovely red dress*
> *It rained on the day you got back*
> *Carrying your trunk down the track.*

The Little Junco

I went crazy the third winter and shot a squirrel that had taken over the attic. That's all I have to say about it except that he had been up there rearranging furniture every night, chewing through the wires I mean to say. At 3:00 AM I said, "There, that's it, he's done for the night." He'd rush then, push, pull, haul, rake, scratch, a little truck of industry. It was coming on a week of no sleep for me. I imagined gnawed wires, rerouted, sparking up light shows in the rafters just to allow for entertainment from a squirrel's new captain's bed of insulation.

My brother made me a mailbox, a copy of the house, complete with red asphalt shingles. I set this on a wintry rail up on the third floor, the balcony east. I set a dollop of peanut butter deep inside the box then used a stick to raise the opposite end.

Every morning the dollop was gone and every evening the chattering fool was on the siding: "That all you got — to feed me! I haven't driven you from the house yet! I will, mark my brown-ass squirrely words! I've been here hundreds of thousands of years, taking what I wish, when I wish and making it mine! You? Lank, white, sickly novice on — what? Two legs! *Chit-chit-chit-chit-chit!*"

I hadn't slept. I saw stars in the daylight and would take off my glasses, pinch the bridge of my nose, turn my eyes from the snow. The rummaging was not present during the day, nonetheless I am sure I heard it. I say attic — it was the spaces between the studs in the ceiling. There was no attic in this house otherwise I could get in there and root out this cousin to the rat.

In the old homestead I found a rattrap and set it up near the vent hole on the third floor where he was entering. I added oily poppy seeds to the dollop and on dizzy mornings found my rattrap with its powerful deadly rusty steel coil, snapped, its slab empty of food and of marauder.

Sixteen nights of listening to rummaging, gnawing, dashing. I grabbed my pillow and blanket and descended to the cold second floor, my knees on the glass of the woodstove. I fell asleep in my purple chair and woke to see a world of snow in shadow out my window, shadow except for the big green spruce where the squirrel chattered in bright sunshine that lit its crown, brave, warm-pelted.

I opened the window, frost poured in as he called from his gathered cones: "You still here? Well, listen up then, Joseph Tenacity. Not your days but your *hours* are numbered! Why? Because I do not to stop, have no plans to stop and stop, will not! Your electrical system is awry and amuck, its tasty coatings stripped bare. Too soon there will be puff, puff, puff, puff — blaze! So you get your Volunteer Fire Department on speed-dial. With a driveway like that they should be up by spring!"

I dialed Willard, my childhood friend who knew fishing and hunting like Van Gough knew his primary colours.

"Willard, Miles. You got any .410 shells?"

"How many do you want?"

Willard arrived and placed eight slim shells in my hand, their lead reassuring, their brass ends cool and attractive.

He spied through my gun barrel, blew down it, snapped it shut. He tried the trigger, his thumb easing the hammer back then forward, his forefinger clicking the trigger. "Your brother Milburn, eh? He was hiding this here? Afraid of it unregistered for the gun registry, was he? Oh, yeah. A few did that. He probably thought what the rest of us thought — that you'd never be back. All right, Miles. Guns are involved and I heard your plea to the judge. But you might have got on to this solution to begin with, eh? Now don't you go nuts over on this hill. Man! Get someone up here! Your point is made!"

Willard disappeared down over the bank of the all-white winter world, leaving me again to the cold quiet six-month shadow of the hill.

But then, chatter.

I approached the spruce and raised the gun, pulled the trigger, and the report that bellowed in my ear said, problem-solved. I sniffed spent gunpowder but the sight of his busted pelt on snow turned the smell in my nose distasteful and I'm sure memorable.

"Sorry, little guy, but you have to know I have one hundred and fifty thousand dollars of Scotiabank blood, bone and back tied up here. And, no job."

It's true, half-mad, me. A half-loon as Milly Molly Meaney put it. I hadn't eaten, hadn't slept, tried all I could to be the compassionate. And I don't want to say this but the employment of firepower felt good, in its problem-solving capacity. But then I understood what Willard had said about having taken this action to begin with — for, when you say you have a squirrel problem it is more often a squirrel-family problem.

I used up all the shells. The last one produced a muzzle flame as I shot in the dark at a fist-sized silhouette in the apple tree, producing a huge bang between me and the long-off drift ice of the sea.

Tim Dickey flashed in the spark. Tim was dead. Dead but below — at the fourteen-foot snow bank, climbing up it over to visit me.

"Don't shoot, Miles! I only came for a game of chess and now you're puttin' a hole in me!"

Sleep deprivation. I saw the dead. What was there was the crown of a tree that rolled in the flash of the muzzle flame, rolled over the massive snowbank in the way Tim did, going back-first over the bank crest before and after any winter visit. What would Tim have thought of my killing the squirrels?

"After exploring every avenue, Miles, you had a problem that needed solving."

As did you, Tim. The Nepali cleaner in Saudi Arabia had warned me — a man living alone is a man who lives with ghosts.

Spring came with bluster and light. The Salt Lake hadn't frozen this year; when I was young, cars had driven on this. There was that Arctic drift ice out there in the Atlantic but it moved off the night of the last squirrel. Let us not conclude any correlation between an unfrozen Salt Lake, an early retreat of drift ice, and the amount of snow that had fallen. I had parked up by the house till December when four feet arrived to say: "You're done with making it to this height, Miles." I parked on the build-up field till February when six feet said: "Better get that car to the road, skipper, and I won't warn you again." I parked at the road from February on but soon gave up freeing passage to the Cabot Trail when the snowplow buried the car for the fifteenth time.

On my March birthday, in what was like a search for the Oak Island treasure, I dug down my standing height and more to touch the roof of the car. And when I found the roof I raised the shovel victorious.

Then the plow came, to blast me with a trainload of snow and slush and ice in chunk and block and house form. The north side of the mountain, it had me; it had always had me. "I'll let the man who put it there come to take it away!" The old guys would say, when religion had its stake here.

On April Fools, I threw my shovel in the woods and overnight, it was buried without a trace. I didn't know who owned it when I discovered it in late summer.

I sledded in or rather "up" my supplies. In Chile they grow grapes on the north side of a mountain. That's Chile, this is just chilly — your nook, at the bottom of big old Smoke. And that snowplow, with its Siberian blade, I would hear wet snow roll, hear slush mortar curl up into the high banks, and think: there's another week of summer that bank will survive into.

But spring came with bluster and light. And I saw from my purple chair the man-sized icicles out my window. I sat by a fire whose green wood I blew my lungs out over and I knew I was feeding those man-sized icicles that dripped with melt. Big as fake pearls, drops came. They fell in the sun, cried in the sun, a sun back again after hiding the winter up over the mountain. The fire roared because I began to burn the fish crate that held the wood and heat lost up the chimney made those icicles grow, grow, grow. They went from man to the size of the buried Chinese Warriors. A sheer arrest stayed, when night temperatures plummeted, when a vague moon walked through.

I ate soup with potatoes; I ate carrots and chickpeas. The mackerel I fished from the Gut in the summer — the sad eyes worn before I cut the heads off — made things like that trouble me. I drank black coffee and my heart race the way it would during cocaine hangovers. I read the classics for the second time: *Ulysses, War and Peace, Moby Dick*. The only good second reading was *Wuthering Heights* — no, strike that. All second time arounds were empty of flavour. They were like Chinese noodles without that little packet of crystals to kill you. No, we're hunters when it comes to books. I read for rhythm, especially, *Finnegan's Wake*. Joyce was supposed to be a guitar player; the guitar's really a drum. I don't know why I was reading these again, relearning how to read maybe, practicing for the red spines. Which I got at.

We live without leaves. I looked out over the winter-worn mountains. But the sun rose, too, hit and said, shut up about that no-leaf situation; I'm working on it. I was on the road with my rake and shovel, my triumphant Rocket back up on the hill. Yes, rake, shovel, pick, water in a bucket, the aggregate harbour gravel in a tub, a puffing bag of cement that weighed a ton and my plastic fish crate I found on the shore in which to mix and knead the concrete dough for the tracks. It was soon: goodbye apple tree, I'm leaving your iron limbs today.

I saw no Charlie. Franklin and Francolene were up on their wire, their faces those of theatre's upper right corner. "Don't you two have nowhere to go? And I know it was you two who ate the burnt rice and made the mess all over the driveway. No — rice was not a peace offering! We three remain at war — understand that you understand a lot. And no hellos about it either." But then, with not a single caw, this murder arrived in whooshes of wings to settle in the maple and beech above the cabin.

I climbed straight for this, to witness the sight, when what followed the murder was a congregation of seagulls one hundred bodies strong. In terrific silence they floated above but at various depths, drifting over bud behind the cabin in a parade that obscured the blue of the sky. I did not move; life can want what it wants of you and of me, but right now I'm not moving. And as strange as it may sound, above seemed a gentle passing of fish, of ocean marvels soaring through the sky.

But eagles clucked; they careened for the harbour. And Juncos clicked, they didn't like me near their cabin-bank nest. An agitated mom had added rhythm to her clicks so I removed my hands from where I viewed her marble-sized eggs, setting back her tapestry of hiding-grass.

"Don't worry, Mom. And as for you Featherheads, stay in the egg. No need to know this world out here."

A double rainbow arched over the bay. I was looking at its configuration in the sun, and in the rain, the rainbows were a mother and its feeding calf. But I felt eyes on me. And I knew what it was.

"Hello, Charlie." And I turned. It wasn't Charlie. Canine, yes, wild, yes. But coyote-big and still as glass atop the bank above the cabin.

"I note your courage, Wolf."

But she vanished in a soundless bound and I was glad to see her able to flee with fluidity.

A truck was at the road, Sammy the Trapper. The man looked to have grown his hair over the winter. Why did I resist him? Why? Because if these folk get a grip on you, look out! Morning, noon, and night they're dropping in with grievances and favours needed. All men are walking wounds.

"Going around the harbour. Want anything?"

"No, Sammy. I appreciate it, though. No, nothing."

The old fellow drove on but slow to show how my unforthcoming ways did not bother him. I must be nicer. Willard's right, too much time on my own. I say that, I'm not sure I believed it.

But another vehicle was below. "Who is this now?" It pulled in and climbed to the built-up field. Here we go, the Highway inspector, Scotiabank coming to ask for blood, bone, and back. Ut oh. Tim's wife. Her kids in, a boy and a girl, not ten. A dark fellow at the wheel. Must be this Philip.

"Hello there," she called, out of the vehicle. I dusted off my jeans, came from the cabin to meet her at the apple tree.

"This is some driveway, I mean — Jesus. You have your work cut out for ya!"

I could smell booze at ten feet. I also saw an eye alert and keen.

"Well, you know who I am. Brenda. And I know who you are, Miles. I couldn't make the funeral." She was going all soap opera in the face. "I planned to. I do got to ask you one thing. It's in a case like this they say there is usually a note. They said nothing was found. You were the first one there. I want to sell the place down here but the property's in his name. There's a hold up. We were separated only. I thought maybe there was something saying who it should go to that you found. We're in the place now. Just to fix it up and sell it."

"No note," I said, keeping my voice clear and even.

"Well then, how do I get the deed?"

"How do you get the deed?"

"Why won't you look me in the eye? Yes, it was his father's property. But I was with him all those years. The bank took his boat, took his license, all his gear. He was in debt up to his eyeballs. I need start-over money. I want to know where my end of things is. He must have said something to you. He was up here. Maybe you can give a statement to the court. Those kids need help."

"No note. He said nothing to me."

She studied my face. She had put on lipstick for this.

"Well, fuck ya then," she said.

"What did you say to me?"

My heart raced and my hands shook. I glanced at her fellow in the car because the next thing I said here was not going to be pleasant.

"I said, fuck ya!" she said. "I know you never liked me. You never approved!"

"I have no opinion of you one way or the other. I hardly know your name."

"Sure, no opinion of the tramp who walked out on your friend."

"Maybe you should have stuck around."

"Don't you fuckin'-well judge me!"

"Why? You're judging me. Oh — we'll go get Miles up on the hill to give a statement to help us take what he had. Since you're asking — he was filled with pain. I knew him as only being a good man."

"I was the one who knew him! You can't speak to me like that!"

"Because you're a woman?"

"Yes, because I'm a woman! That's exactly why!"

"You're also an adult who acts, and chooses. And if you do want to know, I don't believe that everything goes and that all should be forgiven and understood. There's good, there's bad. You decide which you are — now get the fuck out of here!"

She forwarded, stumbled, and punched me in the mouth. I saw her fellow begin to leave the car.

"Come," I said to him, tears stinging my eyes. "I would like that." He got back inside.

"You're a prick," she said, stumbling in her heels. "A weird cuckoo prick up on a hill, all alone."

"Ha! Maybe you should look that bird up!."

The boy and girl watched me as the car backed down the hill. And rat-rat squealed his tires to tear apart the bottom of my road.

The next night, I stood outside the house to catch my breath. I had been to the shore with the chainsaw since dawn, running the machine full bore to take down that miserable old boat shed. All construction materials were in neat packets up from the water. The old stove I hauled up from the beach and set inside the alders. I began covering it in plastic when I remembered I had a house key in the grates. I retrieved that easy enough but there was a book jammed down inside. It was all sooty and I got full of soot but I dug it out. I wiped off the cover: *Trees of Nova Scotia.*

So on my table, from down there was my pencil jar and this book on trees. Tim had hidden it in the stove after filling both back pages. I saw where he had written *Witness* and had signed my name. I took the book and put it in my bookshelf; I wasn't going to read what he wrote or figure out why he had hid it so well, not now.

I grabbed the old eleven-dollar guitar and said, "How's about Old Eleven? Lucky Old Eleven? You like that name? Come then, "Little Junco".

> *I saw a little junco*
> *Outside of my door*
> *He sang a sweet song*
> *Never heard it before*
> *He sang a sweet song*
> *A sweet melody*
> *Oh, little darling*
> *Won't you come back to me?*

Claire

The rest of the Mala Mala gang were off looking for the Big
Five. Africa's lion, elephant, buffalo, leopard, and rhinoceros.
They called for me to join in. I was crouched in the clay with
a dung beetle. I watched him ride high on a dusty brown ball.
The Dutch guide had told me the guy with the biggest ball gets
the girl. This one was rolling his big ball in the orange clay of
the jeep path. Up high, Mister Man beetle was heading her for
town, with the pride of any guy with his first truck. "Ladies!
Check it out! Up here! Look at the ball I have for you — for
us. We can do whatever we want with a ball like this. The little
ones will have real lodgings to be born into. Look at the colour,
the size, the power!"

A female approached. I would guess a female because she
got up there with him.

On the third evening of the sighting of what I thought was
a coyote, I was at the cabin when a smaller coyote appeared.
"Oh, so not afraid this time." It was no coyote but a female
fox, on her haunches, high on the hill above the cabin and
all dolled for a spring evening, I had dug myself a shelf for this
cabin's construction, roots clung from maws and with my snips
I trimmed these. She stayed, her eyes on me.

"Bearer of the gun here, Lady. Of steel traps and poison, a
splitter of atoms."

Along the bank I moved with purpose; with a long stretch of her neck she looked away.

She panted, turned for me; a Circe quality about her. Something was up. Her slender spine waited, her head stayed regal-high and that expensive pelt of hers looked to have been drycleaned. There was that magic tail, her pound of rouge dandelion waiting in a wind-dead field. In her precision and her stillness, she guarded a recoil of youth.

"Are you part-wolf because that is one thick coat. The Animal Rights folks would have something to say if they saw you in that. Vain, I see, to the household-cat extreme. You're the sunset cheetah of the African anthill, that loved the cameras."

She was protecting something. Something that climbed in the grass now past her. Kits. Pudgy kits with paws that worked; there was mewling, testiness.

"All right, all right, I'll leave you all to it."

I slipped into the cabin and with four strides crossed its seventeen feet. I slid open the French door, put a foot on the butterfly deck, and peered around the cabin log ends.

The runt was the last to go. The little thing couldn't climb as the others had, the bank I had dug, a regular cliff for it. But I wouldn't be helping him. No way. Not since that baby moose, Fairy, when the cop arrived last June carrying it up the driveway. Brown limbs dangled and I was sure it was a traffic accident victim. As the cop got closer I saw the long legs that I had thought were arms. He carried a baby moose.

"Here," he said. "See she gets back up on the mountain. Jesus, you have to be part-goat to live up here!"

We stood his moose up, retreated a couple steps from the star of the carnival.

"She was separated from her mother," he said. "And the traffic was building up on your bad turn. I got a camera in the cruiser. Can you snap a picture?"

I snapped his picture and said yes when he asked if I wanted my own with the moose.

There I stood, documented.

"How are you doing up here anyway?" he said.

"How am I doing up here?"

"Yeah."

"I live here."

"Oh, I know. You're Miles. Take it easy now."

He left and the baby moose nudged me. I looked up at the woods, to where the mother must me.

I got the creature inside the cabin because I felt mom was out there and I could easily be killed for being in possession of this loot, the offspring of MacIntosh, the result of his win out on the Clam Flats that day. I say that because I had seen and recognized the moose's mother.

It nudged me again. It was imprinting.

"Get away." I only half-meant this. It was gentle as a lamb, on stilts for legs. A massive head turned, for me, the kind you wanted to speak to. Up to my nose she stood, the prom date who never thought she'd be asked, waiting with you for the music, for the first dance to begin. "See she gets up on that mountain." That cop knew my name, had my picture. He could have got the animal to someone else.

I'd seen the mother that morning. I had seen her before that, one week before, as she swam the harbour, pregnant. Swam for what she thought an island, my park warden brother Paddy had said when I called him. "They need a place where they can have their young, free of coyotes. The coyotes have only been here since 1980. The moose are from Alberta, imported in '47 and '48. It's all sorting itself out."

Have I said how steep it is here? Let's see. Your everyday fridge would need but a touch to travel a full sixty seconds, uprighting and upwronging maybe thirty or forty times before arriving in the harbour. No — that would not happen because of the trees. Yes — it would happen, as after three or four tumbles velocity and gravity would have it ringing off birch, beech, maple; caving in sod, alley ooping over that old car from the fifties joyride down there and crashing finally into the water.

The mother moose and her baby had climbed up over that. The mother had to have worked a day to get the young up a mere ten feet. In the horse world, a colt stands minutes after it's born and runs in thirty. There'd be no running here — slipping and falling maybe, the breaking of a leg.

I spoke to the eyes, "How did you ever get up onto the Cabot Trail when you can hardly stand? Mother? Nudged you? Like you're nudging me now? You're light as a fairy. Can't say the same for your mother. And certainly not your father."

When the duo did make the bank, when they surmounted the guardrail, they could only have discovered the wonderful hard, flat and open world of the Cabot Trail. It must have been then when the traffic ensnarled. I saw the mother gallop up my driveway, scramble for the high woods, blood where she sank in snow deposits hiding in the banks. A brute of an animal, fifteen hundred pounds comes to mind, and stays in mind.

"They'll abandon their young," said Paddy. "No one knows why. The young apparently have no scent. If a cow is separated from her calf, a calf without scent is an advantage against predators. Doesn't work out so well for a mother trying to relocate her calf."

The mother had returned down my driveway but a car had frightened her right back up. Her lungs must been split; she snorted blood. Her fetlock to hindquarter had been torn in her shore climb, or maybe it came from her scramble up the banks I dug here. The lacerations she carried showed strength.

"What am I going to do with you, Fairy? Your mother's hurt; she makes five, six, seven, eight, nine, and ten of me. You're gentle as a lamb. I could probably put you in the car and drive you around the Cabot Trail." I eased her out the door.

Her distress went into me as, in hugs I moved her, upward, tree by tree.

"Where are you, Ma? How do you feel about me doing this, as this is your very life I pick up here and transport — but to you, understand? And for the love of God don't contact that MacIntosh for the search and rescue. I have a question. Will your antler enter my thigh, my back, or just fly straight through my throat?" Quite the commission, cop. That mother weighs as much as two American sedans and so my days end impaled, trampled, trammelled. I remembered the camel's teeth in Oman that spit on me. Big treacherous rat teeth in need of sandblasting — you haven't got those, have you? But you have to be silent as the wind, all creatures up here are. So I won't know what hits me.

I got Fairy to the Tree Ghost Plateau. I consoled her satin head, studied her big brown eyes in a dying June. "Good to get you this far but I'll take my leave of you and your mother, with luck." The Tree Ghost watched. Fairy looked as if to plead: "Please, mister, I don't like these woods. Can't I go with you? You have a house, I'll just hang around. What bother can a moose be? I'll browse your woods. There's no cost. I'm cheap, cheap and quiet."

I saw the heap of dry branches I had stacked when dressing logs for the cabin. I saw the old log pile; a log there had a bird's eye pattern in it, a log whose downing had brought the Tree Ghost to life.

"Bed in the dry branches for the night, moose, alongside the Tree Ghost. It'll watch over you. It's a great sleep.

I was sorry for Fairy, sorry for any animal up here in this spooky dark. But I was underway. She called to me, in a sound like slow running water with a honk in it.

"I'm not what you think, moose. I'm a stranger with a heartbeat, a two-legger who's not been unknown to make a stew out of the likes of you."

I descended, tree by tree and no Ma, thank the Jesus. Then I was in the house, with Paddy on the line.

"Go back up," he said. "With milk."

"I'm not going back up there."

"There was this guy in the Yukon who kept one. He fed it through the fingers of a latex glove. You got honey? You could always keep it by the house, you know."

I went up. In the pitch black. Antler, horn, bone? Blunt blow? Sharp? Will folks see light through me?

I stepped easy, passing the site of the Bee Hill Incident. It was cold, slippery. The village lights were over my shoulder as I carried the milk and honey.

The Tree Ghost waited in the dark, arms missing, his old toadstool maw: "What? Back? Thought I put the fear of God in you? You and all those screaming kids!" How spooky it looked; I got to stop making them.

Then came the slow running water, the honk.

"Shush!"

She was bedded in the brush. I set the bowl on the Tree Ghost's head and got down alongside her, my knees in the mud. Wrapped like a fiddlehead, not wanting any of this, she raised her head.

"What it is you want, then? You got to accept that it's a moose you are and this here is all your home. Take the damn milk, I said!"

I heard a noise, a crackle then all-out *thump* and I lit out of there like a house afire. It surely was the mother so I bothered no tree in my descent, slowing only to alight off that cursed, creepy hill, in an all-out ankle-busting tumble over Charlie's ledge where below the happy village lights shone on a harbour swell.

In the morning I spit toothpaste over my deck east. Thank you out there — east, world. Thank you that that animal got back and maybe after all you can be a big all-out reasonable place, when a person does the right thing, which I had the fortune to do last night. Yes. A big super half-minute of peace comes, with good action.

Wait! What's that I hear? Over there? Oh, oh, no. Above the road, where the cop picked up the booty I heard running water and a honk: Fairy. She was back on the road.

Traffic confusion came. Cameras came out. I think the selfie was born down there.

"Ooooh la la!" said a woman, with an accent.

"Can I cuddle her? Dad? Is she a baby, Dad?"

"Get over here, you!"

"Will she bite, Daddy? She won't bite. Will she, Daddy?"

The Department of Natural Resources arrived in the biggest half-ton ever to come over Smokey. The vehicle did a three-point turn, its brand-spanking-new government-of-Canada tax-paying-dollar tires had tread visible from the deck. *Squeak, squeak.* Two men emerged wearing matching Hollywood-black vests, shutting their doors just so. Hollywood-black gloves came out, each man donning his in grand style. Thumb and forefinger touched wraparound sunglasses. I heard Velcro snapped; shoulder radios broke with transmission. But their work in the shadow of a northern slope was speedy. They loaded up Fairy over a good drawn-tailgate, got her in, down, and secure, gave her a pat, then took my Fairy away. They transported her to a wildlife park in Sydney where she died within week. The cop sent me a photo by mail. It's on the fridge. And so — okay you runt, kit, fox, squirrel, ant! No more hands on any of you!

The kit made the bank and I closed out this night with a stomp at Lucky Old Eleven of "Claire".

> *Oh darling Claire*
> *Of the raven hair*
> *I lie in a hospital bed*
> *Where I was born in Neils Harbour*
> *But now old Neil has me facing west.*

Long As My Wings Will Carry Me

Very well. This was when I was a kid. One spring afternoon I climbed a big spruce not so far from the old house, a tangley old thing no one bothered with — no brother, no sister, cousin, or neighbour. We'll put me at ten years old. I pushed and pushed to pass through a spiky growth that may have never known a human hand. Spruce gum found my mouth. At the top where the branches thinned, cool sea air entered my chest and I saw the ski hill in the sun. I couldn't see the Gut. I must have looked over here. But I was cold so I worked my way around to the crown south.

I had to watch it. I was up thirty feet, an easy fall to my death. My hand grabbed a spiky bit of nature; it was a tough old bird's nest protecting three teeny baby birds. I waved my finger; and blind, they jawed their silent beaks at me. But why was it so quiet out there in the trees? The shadow of a bird in flight spread over me. The bird settled in a near tree and the act stirred up a Greek chorus of cawing.

Black planes shot from the limbs, birds swooped for my face and skull as, scraping, scratching, scuttling, I scrambled down the tree.

I stood on copper ground where a grotesque raven waited on needle and sod.

I ran into the sunlight of our field where my mother was above hanging her wash. "The racket of those crows! I can hardly hear myself think! What are you doing to them? Better not be bothering them. They're a bird that'll remember you."

The next day I went to the tree after a night of pondering over the baby birds. Because how good would it be to have just one would as a pet! I went to the tree and put my hand on a limb and at my sneaker was a little grey sack, two more then in the copper needles. It was baby birds, dead, dead, dead.

My mother was taking her clothes off the line.

"Miles? Promise me one thing."

I looked at her.

"That you'll see the world for me."

I could see the head of a blonde woman come up the driveway. I could see her box of beer and a husky. She rose higher and I saw her cutoffs.

"*Salut*," she called, and I put down my chainsaw where I stood past the built-up field. Her bronze skin was like roasted almonds, her lips red and she had that small nose that Tolstoy said you found only one in a thousand. *Salut*, eh? The Acadians here speak of a Black French, but with her blonde hair she is hardly that.

We met under the apple tree. She had a brown iris and the other slightly hazel. "This is your driveway?" she said. "Why don't you get a company? Is that your cabin? We will go there."

We sat on the butterfly deck overlooking the evening sea east, the Salt Lake and Clam Flats west. Her dog was curled at her feet. The woman was in her childbearing years but which decade I could not hazard a guess; she was no teen yet possessed a teen aspect, a teen to forties aspect. That is another thing beauty's able to do: contain it all, age, race, gender. It does this because it is a freak of nature.

She saw the safety glasses in my hand.

"Cut your tree for your view," she said. "Your beer will wait here. And I." Her dog got up when I rose, sniffed the stone fireplace where a mole lived. "His name's Allouette," she said from where she sat. "I'm Fleur. I research the coyote for the national park. The coyote is here from western Canada. It sexed with the wolf in Quebec on the way. My father was Chinese, my mother was a Russian. I grew in an eentcy town of Manitoba."

She had an accent but, *eentcy*? As in the spider that climbed the waterspout?

"I have heard you need to sell your house," she said. "We will talk. Cut your tree."

I crossed the built-up field. Need to sell my house, eh? No — not that I know of, but what an idea. I was under the power line, in the tall bushes, pushing on the tree now. The tree was notched and I wished to have it drop over the notch; that is to say, uphill — south. I wanted to get back to her. The evening was warm, the sun had been on my shoulders, and I needed proximity — company. She had come over, was above at the main house, studying the structure.

Selling? Why not? The Bank of Nova Scotia will hardly stop wanting its $1,450 CAD, every month for the next twenty years. That's hard enough to pay now. No, I can't really keep it; I never could; I'm poor man and it doesn't look like much changes that from middle age in. I could keep the cabin. She could have the main house and I would always love her but never have to pick up after her.

Her damn legs; they flooded my mind. And the tree's not going over the notch. Cut-offs? Who wears them? Cut off, is how I feel to see them. If I worked for a beer company I would remind the bosses of the cut-offs. It would be the summer campaign. I would win awards.

The problem was, I was one-handing the tree; the idling saw was in the other. I had cut what I thought was a manageable birch, the last tree to obstruct the view from the cabin west — the sunset. Damn it! It listed, in the exact direction I wished it not to.

I put the saw down. But the tree was at the point of no return; any force I could supply to bring it back was futile.

It ached, yawed, and fell onto the power line supplying northeastern Cape Breton. And there it rested on black lines where ten, twenty, thirty — one hundred thousand volts zipped, to and fro!

I clutched at the tree and a buzz passed over the shoddy rubber of the rotten gloves I just happened to have on. I looked at my rubber-soled boots, another article I just happened to have on.

I switched off the damn idling power saw, pulled on the tree with all I had as lime-coloured crown leaves fried as if in a hot pan. A pretty blue fire broke out and I shivered. But my hands in their gloves betrayed me, my arms in their sleeves betrayed me — these limbs dropped as of their own accord, saying: "We will not handle it. We want to live!" I stood, dry-mouthed.

Fleur was at the house in her cut-offs. With an arm up she rested at a corner, and she actually then tied a knot in the front of her shirt, her beer case at her feet.

"Better call 911," she said, with casual precision — with French logic? French, Chinese, Russian logic, whose obviousness made my molars go tight.

"I know the number," she called. "I will enter your house."

In minutes the island was there: both fire trucks, paramedics, notaries — both police cars. The moose-bearer exited a cruiser.

All were below at the bad turn, under the power line where it crossed the road to my place. They were in study of the situation when to rival a NASA launch a fireball sprang from down there to go *ka-boom*! I could not see. Stars were in my eyes.

Allouette the dog had disappeared up in the woods and her coyote researcher went after her. The men below spotted the woman, saw the flash of the roasted almond legs on the evening hill.

"You all right up there, Miles?"

It might have been Sammy the Trapper.

"Who's that wit ya?" he said.

"A naturalist."

"Natural all right," came a reply.

"Miles?" said Sammy.

"Right here. You fellas all right?"

"Is she from the park?"

"Yalp."

"Are you trying to set North of Smokey ablaze?"

"Nope."

"Well you fried her electrical circuit. Hope you weren't touching the tree before she blew. Where did she go?"

"Who? Up in the woods."

The sleekest of Nova Scotia's power trucks left the Cabot Trail then to climb my driveway. Its four-wheel drive transmission bit into the hill like the sharp teeth of a chainsaw.

A young buck got out to wink at me and cross to assess the situation. He sniffed the wind like a pack lead. A bouncer in a bar would take note of his face, its recklessness, its assertion, self-possession. With thumb and forefinger he smoothed back a golden moustache he wore then his arms went akimbo. "We get double time and a half, for this. I can't touch a single thing till the second man arrives. They're all up in Sydney for a wake."

"Yeah?"

He looked at me. "An electrocution."

"Oh."

"Even the monkey falls from the tree."

He took his eyes off me to turn upslope where Fleur wandered. "That your wife?"

"No."

"Daughter . . . girlfriend?"

"Nope."

"I have two little ones and a wife I love but, bai, all that disappears right now. I'd roll off of that and right into my grave, let me look away for the love of God. The weakness, it ain't fit. No, I don't mind coming out for this stuff. Half the calls are this. That a beer she has in her hand?" He spied the case. "Oh, I see. Power goin' out spoiled someone's plans tonight. But you just keep feeding that one the beer and this might turn out all right for you yet." He kept knuckles on a hip. "Russian? I worked with Russians out in Fort Mac. Can't get a boo out of them. Why she up there? You tell her to go? All I know is that that's where I'd be."

Night was its cooling clicks away. Lights to twinkle on the hill across the water did not appear. But then old night did settle and all was as dark as what John Cabot might have seen. It was then the biggest power truck in Cape Breton, one that must have been reserved for urban tragedy, climbed the hill. And, dressed as if for job interviews, four men appeared from the cab.

The eldest, most officious said, "Hell of a road but she held the old truck. That thing could climb the face of Smokey. Sorry about the bottom of your driveway, and your apple tree. You got a rake. Couple of days of raking will have her back. The tree'll grow. Listen. People die all the time around power lines. Half our job is coming out on calls for guys like you, laying trees over power lines. No one owns a home down here, it seems, without doing this at least once. A recklessness endemic is in you guys down north here. Just good thing you didn't touch the tree."

My arms still buzzed.

"Did you?" he said. "Of course — you damn well did. Ah my."

But all men turned. Fleur approached over freshly raked gravel, put an arm against the corner of the house. Her dog was with her. She grabbed her beer case and retreated to the cabin.

"Is she drinking?" said the senior power man.

"Oh, she's on the beer," said the young pack lead.

"Are you drinking?" said the senior power man to me.

"Who? Me?" I said.

"Listen. Down there is sixty thousand watts of killing power coming straight out of Wreck Cove Hydro. Every bit of the power in the Highland lakes is in those black wires. Invite that into your body? Is that what you want? The system sends out two charges. The fireballs that almost blew your local boys apart are charges to free obstructions from the line, broken limbs, crows, seagulls. Crows blow like ducks in a gallery. A third charge shuts down the system and that's when we're called. You got a third down here tonight, congratulations. Congratulations because you shut down power clear cross to Pleasant Bay. A third of Cape Breton is out. I bet you'd didn't think that'd be in the cards when you rose this morning."

He looked around, he looked toward the cabin then across the harbour. "No. It is nice down here in the dark. A Scottish feel's to it, who's got the pipes? Next time, though, as homeowner, we charge you. Tonight we take your name, address, and occupation. Someone got a pen?"

"I got one, I'll write it," said the young pack lead, the family man. He penned the information on the good inside lining of a knee-high boot.

With their chainsaw, it took twenty seconds to get the birch off the line. The crown dropped for the Cabot Trail but did not get far, it got hung up in brush and they left it. I'd be looking at that for years. They radioed in a re-boot. Singed grass was all around; I kicked through this in search of my safety glasses, the smell of burnt leaves and electrical rubbergoing deep in my lungs. After trimming a nice flat top of the birch stump, the men placed my saw on it for display.

The captain stood at the high open door of his truck and looked at me. "You do this before?"

"A guy I had hired did. He was cutting a swath to the house for the domestic line."

"That's right! Deep winter and he knocked a spruce onto the main. That's right, it's coming to me now, this was the property. Yes. You. The guy stuck overseas. What was the name of the guy I talked to, who dropped the tree?"

"Sammy."

"Yes, that's it. His daughter was trapped on the ski lift for five hours. The coldest day in ten years. I saw him in town after and he said that same evening the daughter comes home to say she'd marry the first guy she met, get a warm house and never leave it. This property is no easy property to have." He looked at the driveway. By his dome light he sent a text. At the cabin, a cigarette burned on the butterfly deck.

"Okay," he said. "I'll leave it then, it wasn't you. But this one was. And we don't ever want to meet again, hear me? Not under these circumstances."

Lights were on in the village, Middlehead awoke. The boss closed his truck door and I watched his big quiet burden back down the hill, get turned at the bottom, and head for Sydney.

The hill was lighter with the power truck off it. Across the way village homes on the banks twinkled. Middlehead and the Keltic Lodge with its four hundred-dollar rooms once more were a dazzle of silver streetlights and golden windows. We were in the main house and Fleur came from the bathroom to look up at the cathedral ceiling. "You forgot coziness in this construction." Her arms crossed and I felt as if were we on a car lot. "Insane. You could have died in one fail swoop tonight." Allouette brushed past, he was checking it out.

"I will not buy," said Fleur. "It's too hard living here and that driveway, pfft. You should consider calling the National Geographic Society about the article of the worst driveways in the world. Number one was Nepal. It's too bad they didn't know about you."

I travelled the bank in the near dark, my balance poor on the big nothing began these black woods. My sister Theresa had called, "Victor John had orders backed up, his customers got up and walked out. The Keltic had a dining room full, a golfer convention. The freezers at Doucette's Convenience lost their ice cream. Don't go over around the community for a while." My sister lived two hours north. This is how news travels in the dark.

A crazy crayon moon rose from the sea. It was so much later in the night. But many of these nights had a prohibition on for sleep on the hill. It was 3:01 AM, and I was out on the third floor balcony where below two inky pools crossed the driveway at the broken worksite. It was a mama bear and cub. Suck came; a "ma, ma, ma, ma, ma, ma," — that Chinese sentence about horses. The babbler was the cub.

"You two here because I put out the power and you figure it's safe? Power's back on, boys, so get the hell out of here. Hey!"

I should not be in the woods looking for a mother bear and her cub but the house has the door open and to it is a twenty-second dash. I climbed to the third floor. You sometimes have only to wait for inky shadows to cross your path and then sleep will find you to freeze you out. Though, it does not.

On the second floor I snapped on a low light. I grabbed Old Eleven and by the woodstove gave a stomp of "Long As My Wings Will Carry Me".

> *Every night outside my door*
> *There's a little bird that sings*
> *That calls to the woodland*
> *For the love she's suffering*
> *She says please come with me*
> *And we will fly away*
> *Just you and me together*
> *With the sun to guide the way.*

After the Funeral

I woke to screaming, to my eyes welded to the ceiling. I turned
to see that all about my world was deep dead white winter and
here I lay in bed. The window above my head was open because
the green wood of the airtight had been asphyxiating me. The
curtains ends, frozen by my sleeping exhalations, knocked.
Another cry! I got my head up for the cold air entering.

Yes, a bleak black dead old world out there with only the tiny
children of stars huddling for heat by the Big Dipper dipped low
in the sky north. Had it come from the big spruce, just there,
the one that the squirrels had liked? Could it be a wintering
baby eagle stuck in the branches and trying not to fall, or to
fall more? Black cones were bunched like spent shotgun shells
when again there came, " . . . *Grr awaa iii ahhh iii . . . UUAU!!!*"

I saw it. A lone lynx was crossing my winter slope, stopped
under my black window, aching below for its kind. It left my
bed and with feet bare crossed to the room east; on its balcony
I stood atop freezing asphalt I had nailed down to offset
creeping ice. Yellow eyes shone from the hardwood slope on my
silhouette high above here on the balcony. I saw the ear tuffs
and could smell urine.

Returning around the bad turns at the ski lodge tonight a
cold summer fog entered the beech and maple. I was coming
from the old property where in the rain I had dug up a pine I
planned to plant. On my outgoing ride there, I had picked up

a hitchhiker. He was sixteen or seventeen, had a good whisker and emotional brown eyes.

"How you making out, Miles? Good?"

I looked at him.

"Nah, you don't know me. I'm Lawrence Dardanelle. My old man's Phillip."

"Oh, Phillip."

The young guy was as skittish as a stray dog. He put on no seat belt, wore a T-shirt and jean jacket and had extra long legs. He balled up his hands as I turned up the heater. He looked off at the mountains when we came out of the bad turns but then deeply into road of the straight stretch at the Clam Flats. He himself seemed to be operating the car, the way his face was fixed forward and all out there was more than asphalt, centre lines, and gravel shoulders.

"If you were to talk to a young fellow like me," he said. "I suppose you would tell him to get the hell out of here and do something with himself." I could see he was sort of looking at me and was eager to hear the answer here. It would be deliberation for later, on the seashore; on the road shoulder in his jean jacket; while getting drunk with friends in the spruce woods near the parish dance.

"Nothing wrong with either," I said. It was no answer at all. "Not a bad life to stay., too" He listened and nodded like an ancient.

I let him out at the old homestead and he walked down over the hill to the village in the rain. He was entering a place a little foreign, his people being from outside the village. Something told me he was about to make a move, even tonight, that home was no option.

So, after getting my pine and heading back, out on the road at the bad turns by the ski hill I saw the orange kits. I screamed on my rickety brakes, skipped to a ski-stop, and rolled down my window.

"Off the road, yas maniacs! Where's your sense? Git, I said!"

I climbed my wet hill as a three-quarter damp moon in my rearview pulled herself from the sea, which, according to my studies, made the time of this event fifty minutes later than that of the previous night.

Charlie was on his ledge. "Your kids are running amuck! I don't have the privilege, no, but aren't you an errant pop? Go ahead. Tell me now how marvelous it is to have them. That I will never know love till I have one of my own. Good, good. Quiet, quiet. I guess you're all out tonight, the moon's making loonies of you. Your mate-tress was also up the road as I was pulling in."

He came within a foot of me and I looked in his eyes. But the phone rang and after the hitchhiker, I said, why not — answer it.

"You got a fox over there?" came the male voice.

"Who's this?"

"National Park. Louis LeFarge, Park Warden. You can't feed foxes."

"Who's feeding foxes?"

"Listen, I'm with the Cape Breton Highlands National Park and we got word you're keeping a fox there you call Darlene. I know you aren't in the park. But all animals around here are under the park's care, however it is they drift in and drift out of it."

I looked out my back window expecting to see Charlie step dance on the bank, cross his arms and do a highland fling because that is how life is.

"You're in charge of all animals?" I said.

"I know you don't live in the park. You also know I have a job to do."

"I'm not even close to the park."

"No, you're not. But we can't have people feeding wild animals. What if people starting feeding bears and take bears as pets? If they start feeding then breeding coyotes?"

"You couldn't call on a person at a regular hour?"

"We've been trying a regular hour, since last fall! You can't be reached during the day and there's no answering machine. We're all wondering why you even have a phone. The community sees your lights on at night, hears your chainsaw. We know you're there. A fox is no pet, no matter how cute. A wild animal's a wild animal."

I didn't get upset; I don't. I did wonder how word travels. The power outage, it must be; that coyote researcher Fleur and her dog, Allouette.

I promised Park Warden Louis LeFarge I'd feed no more foxes and I put down the phone. I stared out at Charlie on his ledge and tore off a big piece of bread. But a raindrop struck the windowpane and in a minute all hell broke loose.

Up from the Atlantic there lifted a gale and beech, birch, and maple leaves of the mountain spun in World War I propellers to take off from their limbs. Hailstones the size of golf balls struck. The Rocket got it good. Quivering rain in sheets like shaken Plexiglas fell and shrank sight of the sea.

Charlie looked at me through it. He shook off the water and slunk away.

I ran from third floor to basement, shutting windows and doors. Wind resisted me; it glommed onto curtain fabric and sucked it out to have it flit like dragon tongues. This was a hurricane from Africa by way of Texas by way of the New England and I told myself, please listen to at least the forecast.

But the windows were closed and I stood on the second floor, at the glass to the balcony east.

An owl was out in that driving rain. Like a decoy it waited in the big spruce, sister tree to the ant-chomped. The owl was down at the foot of the driveway maybe looking up at me by the light. A black owl, where all howls. The wind whipped up whitecaps on the harbour; the sea was the world biggest washing machine, and when I turned back for Howl the Owl he was still nailed by the feet to a branch of the spruce. So northern, so lonesome he waited. But a whoosh struck an eave complemented by a big bang round back. I sped down to the back door to see Charlie's bank caved in. To see rainwater and leaves and clay spill down over the Rocket; a tree lay over its roof.

The deluge had missed Charlie's ledge but had transported an island of poplars to seal my car door north.

I was out in it, trying my door and got it open but then ducked as a real tree, a maple, came piling down. The power behind me was extinguished and limbs cut my nose. I looked to the village — all was black. Good! Not me! We can get on with life! Other things put the power out!

Inside I felt around on the bookshelf and found my flashlight. I returned to close the back door when my flashlight picked up flapping, as in wings, black, on my floor. "Hello." Franklin. The poor old wretch had snuck in having decided to forego the rain for any bit of human world to save him. He pressed at the firewood stack of the little porch, was soaked and dignified, his bad wing resting on the floor.

"Where's the missus? You left her out there in this? You and Charlie, bai — quite the spouses."

"Hello."

I held the door open but he wouldn't scram, only waddle closer to the inside wall where he leaned like a drunkard. The end of his days neared, I figured. "Dear Old Bent Wing, I write to you tonight in concern for your health. Stay, then. Just don't cash in your chips though, not here, hear? Nice thing to wake to." Then the bird let out a caw ten times that of any prior and it pretty near deafened me. I held the flashlight like a cop ready to strike a villain.

"Don't you do that again! Jesus, bird — I'm alone here!" I tore him a ration of bread and got him jug water then went straight up to bed to offset the cold and damp that fell over the land and got stuffed in the house. I listened, my socks, T-shirt on, listened to heavy timber creak at the corners, slighter timber moan in the walls.

But there was weight was at the foot of the bed and I kicked at it. It hopped. "What in the blue . . . ?" A candle was beside me but matches were downstairs. I located my glasses, found the flashlight.

Holy jumping old dyin' Jesus! The crow was in bed with me! Nice forebode.

"Git, you! Git, you!"

Franklin hopped down and went off with his damaged wing to cross the plank floor.

"Keep going, keep going. Staying in, one thing, but no bird on the bed! No bird up here!" My mother was petrified of birds in houses. It meant death.

I heard him take the steps and it reminded me of the night the mouse set off the trap in the kitchen and alive it carried the contraption behind the fridge. *Snap, scrape, snap*, I heard and had to get up. Not warmed up for heavy work I hauled out the fridge and saw him disappear in a wall. I went back to bed and in the dark heard him free himself and set off with his crucifix, step by step, ascend to me to present to me what I had nailed him to. The heart wasn't there to get up again and it was so cold. I listened till he stopped, thank the lord, checked my bed that was still too cold to get out of. In the morning I took care of him, where he lay.

Now in my bed I only saw a roof twist off in a hurricane, I saw only half the house break down over me and we all wash out into the harbour, Franklin, me and the timber; watch how we ease for the sea. I lay under summer covers listening for Franklin, lifting my head every few minutes to see that he wasn't there at the foot of the bed.

In the morning I found a radio and turned it on. Franklin opened an eye to my standing above him; he discovered where he was, nestled in against firewood in my porch.

"Bird. You're refreshed. But here's a tip, don't go jumping on people's beds."

"Hello . . . "

"I'll hello ya."

He had leaned back at my speech, looked longer than wide, greyer. I got my boots on and pushed at the door, pushed at it and at the limbs barring it. I got out in the air to twist past the debris for full daylight.

Franklin waddled in my wake. "You hurt?" I stood in mud and didn't see him for a second when, clear out of the blue, a second set of wings swooped down. Francolene. She cawed, all right, cawed and cawed and he lifted off to sail shakily down over the driveway for the Cabot Trail and its power line. She followed, barking all the way at this philandering of his. She got in against him, could surely feel house-heat off him. Franklin, old boy, you'll hear it today. You are a bird in the doghouse.

A storm-spent morning loaned me its lightness. I breathed largely. Down at the Gut, in company precision, came the crash of breakers over the sandbar. A bright sun from atop the bill of Smokey lit Middlehead's green fields and the Keltic Lodge wore on its red roof in tinsels of rain; sunshine warmed white shingles, brick chimneys, American sedans in the parking lot.

I needed my chainsaw. The maple had buried the Rocket. The landslide jammed the passenger door up to the roof. Leafy limbs covered metal, glass, rubber, antennae, license plate, and both racing mud flaps.

At the cabin on the butterfly deck, on a corner rail where I filed the chainsaw tooth by tooth, I saw paw prints in the wet of the warming Cabot Trail. I set down my file.

I followed the prints to the highway ditch below the cabin south whereupon I fell and cursed out the boots I wore. I rose, got along a bank with a maw that darkened in alders. I clutched these and up inside on sunlit-dappled clay, on a little stage was a furry lineup. Five kits and a mom.

Silent as snow the lineup stared to start: Act 1 Scene 1 CHORUS *This is all we got for a home. This is where we live and we know nothing more than to hide and to eat and to wait when danger it appears.*

Heads backed off but the camera lens — me — was too much of a draw. "Here, yas weathered the storm, did yas? All right, who wants a name?" I had found the den where the mom could only wait, severe and tall, exit stage left and exit stage right barred from them. I had them cornered.

I whispered that, of course, of this location no soul would I tell. "Where's Charlie Pops? No white tail with a black ring to make the family album complete? Must be busy day and night now, to feed you lot."

There was a burst of gambol and two kits in a perfect ball tumbled over the toe of my boot.

"Get up ya fools, 'fore yas are kilt! Before you take me down, in this slipperiness! And get in off the road!" I let the mother do it. I left them to their red clay den, in the glinting Atlantic light after a summer hurricane.

I went back to that den one dozen times more. All stayed empty, only the lonesome truth of survival sat up there inside, which is to trust none. Instincts are fine for hunting, mating, even imprinting. But survival techniques. They're the mother's department.

I read the last page of the autobiography of Benjamin Franklin. "All must go back in its place," he had said in the book. In all these books only one or two sentences ever spoke. I picked up the volume and put it back on the shelf, Volume 1. I took down Volume 2. What's that? Four inches, less the Five Feet of Books? Was this old Milly Molly Meaney even alive still?

With my shirttail I cleaned my glasses. What's this one? *The Apology of Plato.* Now what's he apologizing for? What did he do wrong? Ah my. Plot lines, in these lives of ours. We grip the pen, all right, a pen we only think we have. I was working through my father's journal, too: "The National Park came, got a hold of property next door for nothing, and put up a cow-catcher, a set of steel rails along the ground. Our cow got in it and broke its leg. My father didn't have money for another cow . . . "

Poor old Dad. I closed out the night with a stomp at Old Eleven of "After the Funeral".

He handed me the violin
He slackened off the bow

A Hard Old Love Amongst Scavengers

He said it's all your now
I won't play it no more
Your mother's gone
My heart is broke
I feel it in my hands
Do you think you might
Play it when you can?

You Always Bring a Ray of Sunshine

A winter harbour scratched frozen paws at a black ceiling of ice that covered it. Above whipped a wild winter wind from the highlands, wind escaping for the seaweed dirty floe to please carry me away, for I don't know where to blow. The bizarre departure did not sustain itself but like a cut curtain dropped long before the Gut. This revealed the two coyotes trotting across the scene, a lustrous pair of pelt and starved grace on the eternal mission. I was at the woodpile, in a torn red T-shirt and Brazilian leather slippers, throwing stew out for hard-up crows. Turmeric had killed the meal, beans and rice burned bullet holes in the snow. I listened to choral dogs across the harbour on a bleak village bank. The coyotes hauled in their reins. I blinked out snow beginning to fall, could see a dog break from a property and beat straight for its silent cousins. The coyotes skipped from the well-fed pursuant, stopping when the lazy fury gave up chase. The dog saw that the pursued had stopped and this renewed its rage, he turned and kicked hind paws to come again. This cat and mouse game crossed to my side, to below the big pine of the eagle's nest where I heard the pack rip it to pieces.

Late one night while driving the Rocket I saw grim death too clearly out on the bad turns of the ski hill. I gathered it off the road, a kit. Further on I saw a coyote, wolf-sized, relaxed on haunches.

I climbed the hill and once inside turned on the radio for the forecast. "Suspect arrested for armed robbery at the 258 Charlotte Street Scotiabank branch one day after the hurricane that wreaked such damage on the island. Eighteen-year-old, Lawrence Dardanelle will appear in court . . . "

I stepped out on the balcony east to see that a truck equipped with overhead lights had crept up the hill. I went to the back door and a big guy was on the step. "I'm who called," he said.

It was Park Warden Louis LaFarge, a younger man than I would have guessed. He was lean like a 2x8, clean-cut, deer-eyed, sharp-chinned, and in the middle of it all a warrior chief's nose. He wore a T-shirt, jeans, and sneakers and had a choker around his neck. He rubbed his arms, had a rubbery aspect about his frame.

"Cold?" I said.

"Slap bang to death! Your brother, Paddy, said you had an apartment. That cabin over there'll do, I don't give a sweet fuck. Broke up with my longtime girlfriend — one. Got in a fight at the bunkhouse — two. I had to sleep in the truck last night — that's three, and four. I thought this was summer. The gas died at midnight. Got some of that and the heater broke. I couldn't tell ya if a person has a job anymore. Someone said a remark about my people."

"Who are your people?"

"The Newfoundland Indians."

"The Beothuk were decimated."

"Mi'kmaq. Someone was shootin' off about them coming in the highlands and shootin' all the moose in the park. The boss had me call you. You can have eighteen foxes. Give them all names and social insurance numbers." He looked around in the way Franklin had, when he knew I wouldn't drive him from the door.

125

"That the stove?" he said.

"Go to it."

He even moved like a plank. "Yalp, night in the truck. I don't know why it got so cold. Shouldn't be in a vehicle when temperature drops." At the woodstove he studied the harbour and the sea.

"So?" he said.

"What? Stay?"

"I'll pay you rent. But say no and I'm pulling for straight off the island. Not looking back till 'Welcome To Cape Breton' is in my rearview. Hello Happy Valley. Load of sad cargo on its way back home. I go by Looie. Two *o*s and an *ie*."

I offered Looie stew from the pot at the back of the stove. He scooped himself up a bowl and ate it where he stood. He took the carrots in his molars.

Rent, I thought. I did have zero money. And if I spend another night up here alone I'm going to lose it. Yet that became the thing to hold on to right now.

"If you need references," said Looie. "We can forget the deal rate now."

"I just don't want to use language that upset you."

"What? Micmac? Oh, I don't care about that."

"Take the house then."

"Come on, bai. I don't want a man's whole house!"

"That's what I got. Six hundred good? I got to work on the cabin anyway."

"Bai. Just when you had enough of this beaten-up old problematic world." He set his spoon and bowl in his left hand and with his right hand shook mine.

"Tanks, bai."

"Sure, Looie. What else am I gonna do? You know, I got a fox."

"No, I don't," he said with his big pair of eyebrows coming together like conspirators.

His gear was in the truck. He had all his belongings with him. We got it in two loads.

So I carried my blanket over to the cabin and grew my beard, the big native Looie LeFarge from Labrador had the main house. He was at one of the rare points in life, he said, when a person's world has him on trial, when slander and accusation abound and all the defense lawyers are out divorcing people because the money's better. Looie drove the nicest truck I ever saw, a big Ford 4x4. It set off the whole hill, turned it from the attempted to the complete.

In the evenings he would come to the cabin, creep across the slope like a hunter in need of what he traps.

"You steal up, Looie."

"What's that supposed to mean?"

"What's what supposed to mean?"

He passed me a big ham and cheese sandwich then bit into his own.

"You're just quiet in your moves," I said.

"I don't like people banging pots when they come upon me, I don't bang pots when I come upon them."

"Looie? What are ya, six feet? You remind me of one of those big weathered planks they set on scaffolds to work from."

"Six foot one and a half. Been that since fourteen."

"And your heart's all broke?"

"Shattered, like a seven-year-bad-luck mirror."

I was working on my shower tower, I informed him, an eight-foot high, ten-foot wide curved bit of stonewall. I didn't tell him I had to stop with the driveway because he was up and down it in his vehicle all day long and you can't cure concrete in that situation.

From the changed activity, the digging in the bank, the mixing of concrete here, the placing of stone here, my hands took on the grip of logging hooks. I was having trouble with the sandwich. But part of the trouble was with the accepting of the sandwich, a meal someone had taken time to make for me. We looked at my digging in the mountain.

"The stone provides the coverage," I said.

"For what?"

"For the toilet."

"You're building a toilet? Nice size arse!"

"That's what I've been saying, shower, toilet. People who come to the big house over there all see this cabin and first thing they ask is, 'There a bathroom over there?' You want a bathroom? I'll build you a bathroom if it'll stop the question, I'll build you one of Smokey granite, mountain timber, and the stained glass I found at the Baddeck dump. All will face a big blue ocean east and never will there be such a squat when you see what you see over from the one-way window in the curved door."

"I suppose."

Looie looked me in the eye. "Tanks, bai, for letting me stay. You seem to me like a fella who needs his peace and yet you give her up just to help me out. I know you fuckin' well did so don't you say otherwise."

"Looie, this cursing."

"I know, I'm on it. Yalp, long distance relationship I had with this one. This here's the first rest I got in years."

"Well you're young enough to get it all going again."

"You too." he said biting his sandwich, looking away.

"LeFarge?" I said.

"Farge, Forge, Farge. Farge, I guess. They told me you were all over hell's creation, Miles. That you were a sniper in the military."

"Ho! Me? My brothers are in the Navy, I'm no sniper."

"Me? I was to Saint John's, once. Where's this here Darlene they all talk about?"

"Charlie — who talks about?"

"No one."

I worked the back of a teaspoon at the grout. The plan was to raise the wall six inches a day. I was up a foot and a half. I didn't like people watching me work because I never knew what I was doing. The thing I had is no hesitation to get going on things. People mistook that for knowledge. Looie had this quiet about him so he was okay. But when you looked at him to mutely question him on this — with silence of your own he would produce this big-acre smile and an old barn-saw set of teeth would come out: "What the fuck did I do now?" His voice came as if through a drainpipe and yes, every chance he got he swore. He was first to tell you that, and his telling seemed his way of putting himself in the clear. Your acceptance made you a bosom friend. "Goin' to hell, anyway," he'd say. "I don't give a fuck, it's just sounds."

A meditative look would spread across his face. He had a rich inner life, perhaps. He wanted guidance but could give it too. "And you don't ever have to worry about me bringing a woman here, Miles. Enough damage is done there to have repairs go into the next century. I'm keeping my distance from them. First time in a year and a half a person's smiled. Is that a life?"

Two nights later, Sammy the Trapper's truck signalled for my driveway. Oh, Sammy — contact with the hermit on the hill

129

at last, eh? It was not Sammy. It was his good-looking daughter. I rose from my toilet wall, up three feet now, as the girl drove straight up a hill few would attempt. Looie was in the house. He had told me in the afternoon he had seen a girl at the post office, who blushed when they passed on the walk.

"Hear me now," he had said. "Contact started, contact finished on that walkway. Keeping my word. Staying clear of them." Oddly, he didn't swear in this exchange and his big brown eyes contained all the tannin of a good spring runoff. Something's good when your eyes fill with colour.

The truck door closed. She was on the step, she was inside.

"Collecting for the SPCA," said Looie, crossing the slope fast, Sammy's truck easing off the hill and onto the Cabot Trail. "Cats," he said, a big knot in his forehead. "Me? I hate the fact we share a planet with them. I gave her twenty bucks. I wanted to give her a pack of .22 shells. Holy Mother, look at the view you got from this toilet shower! I wasn't down here, on the flat! By the old dyin' Jesus, bai! Person won't be reading no Reader's Digest here!" He turned from the view like he'd seen it a thousand times then and came and stood above.

"I'm ruint," he said.

"How are ya ruint?"

"Love ruint."

"Then you're ruint."

"Am I? Miles?"

"She's Sammy the Trapper's daughter."

"Granddaughter, she said."

"Really?"

"Can't say I like the sound of your reaction there. But I guess we all got to be someone's granddaughter — son, I mean. She a teenager, Miles? I'm thirty. Trapper? No, they don't carry guns or nothin'."

"A man who wants a good night's sleep should not marry a beautiful maiden."

"Who'd want sleep? That lying beside ya?"

I worked a stone map of Canada in the wall. I had Looie insert Newfoundland in the mortar. Labrador was part of the big Quebec slab.

Looie slipped back to the house and returned, keeping quiet while I finished with my teaspoon. He produced two bottles of beer from his back pockets.

"Fuck, these are opener kind," he said.

I used my teaspoon to open the bottles.

"What am I supposed to do?" he said. "I'm askin' ya, Miles."

"You mean besides shaming every tree on the slope with your cursing?"

"It's a psychological habit."

He wore no shirt but that choker never left his neck. Barefoot, heart heavy. He sat in the tea berries of the slope and lit a Colts cigar.

"How old is she really? You know, Miles?"

"I grew up here, Looie. But I'm new to all the game here too."

"High school, I'm thinking."

"Better than junior."

We touched bottles and drank. "Junior," he said. "Ah my poor, poor heart. Stripped bare on a steep bank in the evening sun."

"In Yemen they marry at fourteen."

"That all she is? You think?"

I looked at Looie, the big face of the young chief. I set down my bottle and got on a rubber glove, worked the back of the teaspoon. "Looie, a knot's in your forehead a boy scout couldn't untie. Get it together. It'll go or it won't go."

"Who learnt ya that? Buddha? But it helps. Mind if I bring beer over? That big house and beautiful view got me in a prison, with this."

Evening came swift. Looie and I drank. I carried over an armload of the red books from the house, then a bookshelf to put them on. Looie sat by the fire on the flat behind the log cabin and checked his phone. Steaks sizzled on an old oven grill, the fire in the drum of a clothes dryer. We jammed potatoes in foil down in the coals and didn't know how we'd retrieve them. Louis had the box of beer at his feet. Stars shone through the crowns of scorched maple where I had too big of a fire on once. Gold and silver boxes of light ran from village windows into the harbour and the expensive Keltic Lodge rooms twinkled across the bay.

We studied my curved wall. "Miles. Not many get to do what you're doing."

"What? Come up with work for themselves into the next century that doesn't pay a dime?"

"Yes — you're on it like a full-time job. No, it'll pay. Any investment of time has value."

"You mean like at VLT lottery machines?"

"If you strike it."

We clinked bottles. The truth was about seventy hours a week was going into the projects I had lined up. I was just no good at walking away from something started. It was costly. I didn't know the end game. Fire sent smoke out to our chairs and had us rotating the drum. But every minute I felt I should be doing something; early morning traffic to schools flowed by here, people off to government jobs, people off to positions at seasonal tourist operations — it all caused me guilt. The flowers, the birds, the bugs: all were busting their way and earning their salt. Salt? The fishermen were the ones to really wreck me. I saw them leave at 4:00 AM and come back earlier and earlier each afternoon now that they were getting closer to season's end. Quotas met; catches sold; larders lined — a line was in my life: a credit line, one slamming to a complete end. I had an appointment at the Scotiabank next week to consolidate loans. No job, no wife, no son. And I drank my tenant's beer.

I stirred up the fire, dropped in a couple sticks. But neither of us talked about what he didn't have. The early stars had grown small up past the singed reaching maples. Our necks craned; northern lights licked at the stars.

"Jesus," said Looie. "Liven her up here. We're like two old prospectors that haven't talked to anyone else in eighteen years. I heard you play a guitar over here last night. Get that out and give us a tune, for Jesus sake, 'fore we go and end her all down in the harbour."

Prior to the mosquitoes carrying us off I got in a stomp at Lucky Old Eleven, out in the dirt, "You Always Bring a Ray of Sunshine".

> *You always bring a ray of sunshine*
> *Whenever you walk in the door*
> *When I see you*
> *Oh springtime it breaks through*
> *You're my sunshine*
> *I never ever wanna let ya go.*

Johnny Lillington

I know it was early summer because the boats were removing their lobster traps from the fishing grounds. I was digging beds for the driveway tracks when I struck a big rock that had to be down three feet. I thought it would take ten minutes to extricate but ten minutes became the morning. When we were digging my father's grave my nephew Nelson had said, "If you can split her with a crowbar she'll come out!" I split nothing but wrenched and hauled and yanked and heaved, crowbar bangs shaking my arms from their frame. The rock had the iceberg quality: I thought it was fifty, it was more like four hundred pounds; I thought it was medicine-ball size; it was more like an industrial sewer tank. With crowbar, with pick, with time forgotten and a shovel handle snapping, with the use of the wheelbarrow on its side, I got that mammoth wisdom tooth out.

At midday the site was dark in the cover of summer leaf but some sun got down in the hole and it lit a seam. I raked what looked like gold. But no one finds gold here so I pulled the flashy material out of the way and was looking for hardpan, a term my father used for the rock that was under most topsoil here, a bed you can build on.

A colour appeared with more vibrancy than gold, an orange, an orange that was moving. I crouched to see a mess of bugs, the tiniest I had ever seen. I wiped my glasses to make out their legs. Their colour had a brand spanking new quality to it and I wondered how eyes can inform us yet of a new tint. "What's the function of you guys, way down here in a big black hole under a huge rock? And in this grand sweeping world, why orange for a bug folk seldom seen? You've been all this time too, under this rock, hurting none yet with all the zest of the rest."

I got one on my finger and was sure I was seeing a thing none had, not on this hill. But that is the pride of the backyard. You think the tally is complete till you find some minuscule industry like this and are sure it is not. The little orange bug told me my life had not started nor would it, so give up such contemplation. Move your legs, work with others. To communicate why any of us are so orange or pink or blue or black or yellow in so dark a world is word wasted. I flicked him in the dirt and covered in the hole. In this section, no hardpan, but that would be okay.

The days were warm. Looie and I ran the harbour and swam the Gut. We laughed and spat salt, climbed in our wet sneakers over beach rocks and past broken fishing gear. From the Cabot Trail, at the base of the log cabin we drank from a trickling brook.

"What do you call your run, Miles? The Tin Man? That's good because that's what any of us are. This brook here's barely running but drink it. It won't kill ya. Cupful a minute is flow enough, according to the Park handbook. Who cares if a bear took one, up there."

On his balcony north we downed beer and worked on a deck of smokes.

"There's something I did want to ask, Looie."

"For a loan?"

"To cross the island."

"This island?"

"The Highlands. Straight to Cheticamp."

"There's a whodanger move, he who don't give a dang."

"We can we leave behind the house."

"Why here? Oh, power outage. Shying away from the public."

"Oh, no."

"Oh, yes. I'm from Labrador, bai. Wide berth of people, best thing a man can strive for."

"Looie, you haven't cursed once in this whole conversation."

"I know. What the fuck's wrong with me?"

He picked up his pack of cigarettes. "Why do I even close these? Here, smoke? Bai, I got to give up this running shit. No, easing up on the cursing is because this other one says I swear too much, too. Bai, last thing I wanted was to get rate back into her with someone. Let me check with her."

"Check with her for what?"

"The hike! I keep expecting that trapper to come down over the hill every night and put a slug in me while I sleep. The hatchet's by my bed." He opened for us two bottles of bottled moose but we got drunk anyway.

It looked like Christmas morning for rich kids. Looie had gear out all over the second floor, compasses, GPSs, sleeping bags, gas stoves, plastic sheets, tent pegs, aluminum pots, plates. I thought of Benjamin Franklin's, everything back in its place: "To make an account, of what we got," said Looie. He stood his plank height and told me to come have a look at the topographical map he had out over the kitchen island.

"Did I tell you I love it?" he said to me.

"Camping?"

"No. This. Here. The land. When the snow comes and locks us in forever watch and see how I get up that mountain with my snares. Snares for me are the titty bottle for the baby. I can't sleep at night when I got a fence of them up. Key is not to set too many. That never works."

He looked at his phone; a text had come in. "No mobiler, eh, Miles? You? Don't change that, me son. Do you know that everyone in town knows we're going? Where's my liquor flask — Jesus H. Harold Christ! I got to go through all that mess again! Because we ain't going, I don't find my flask!"

We stood outside the house at 6:00 AM in our Klondike packs, drinking just one more coffee and polishing off the last two smokes.

"I know one thing," I said. "These packs ain't the lightest in the world." I had to get mine off my shoulders. He got his off. We looked at the packs, the mountains, the clouds, put out a hand.

"Leave word with anyone?" I said.

"I left it."

"The park?"

"Park don't need to know everything. I have my work cell."

"Looie? Take this stick."

"I don't use walking sticks, Miles. Give it, then."

We bent and leaned into the mountain. I got on Charlie's ledge and, winded, pulled my thumb from my pack strap. I kicked mud off Tim's walking stick. "Feels like the shuttle mission — going straight up like this. Looie, this is where he sits."

"You told me, Miles. I been watching for him every night."

It took us twenty-nine and one-half minutes to get to the Cradle. Our lungs were on fire and the sweat had come through our shirts. Another half hour took us to the crest of the Highlands and by all bright-eyed accounts we faced now seventy-two kilometres of more or less flat woods.

"Mile's done," I said.

"Looie's done, too — don't say that, Miles! Count the distance and we'll never get there. Oh, let me get this goddamn pack off! Hatchet, cast-iron frying pan, American police-beating size flashlight — where we going, the Arctic Circle?"

We sat in a clearing. Our packs behind us like sofas.

"Yes. She's one hell of a journey already," said Looie. "What shape is a man in, anyway?"

"The mountain killed us," I said, and swatted a prehistoric-sized horse-fly.

"That. The thicket. Marsh. That thorny pasture that just crossed from hell into purgatory. Your boots."

"Hot."

"Too hot."

"Flies."

"Fuc, fuc, fucking flies — I guess there's flies! They're manufactured for the whole world, up here! Pst!! And I just ate two! Another's got an electrical storm worked up in my ear!"

"Want to say fuck it?"

"Fuck what?"

"The trip."

"Trip! Miles! I can still see your house!"

"Don't look at it, then."

"Your decision."

"Thing is I never gave up a journey," I scratched a welt the size of a golf ball.

"I don't know, Miles. That's a lot of times, the problem."

We climbed north and entered a strange woods with good flooring of moss and needle. We were well past the ski hill and soon rapelling over a waterfall. A good hundred feet was the drop to the base and we did it smiling.

Getting the gear back together, we marched through falling foothills of pine to arrive at a rushing riverbed and enjoy in a rushing valley wind a clear view of our surroundings. We talked no more about whether we were going or not; the journey was informing us. We struck camp on hard sand where tannin water slid past. A gorge was just up the river, the water coming through it loud.

"If we get at least one night in, no one will say too much," said Louie. We pulled at branches and small trees caught in the river stones, for a fire. There was a mess of debris, no trouble at all getting burning material.

"This stuff comes down in the spring runoff," said Looie.

"You worried because you're a warden?"

"Worried — about aborting the mission? This life is mine. I thought it was. But walking out in the dark, would be good, too. No one sees ya in the dark."

"Then what?"

"Then what, I don't know. Hide a couple days with a case of beer and a couple of movies. There bears up here?"

"Looie! You, asking me? You're the professional!"

"But you grew up here. Yes. There are bears here, I don't need to ask."

We hoisted our packs high in a tree but a ways down from our camp, down past the rushing wind off the river. Out on the stones we ate big pork chops and with a Minolta, Looie took pictures of the fire. A moon came over the ridge and we sat on flat stones near the hard sand. Clicks, groans, and footfalls made it through the rush. This may have been tricks of the water.

Looie looked into the dark woods, "Heart of darkness, there. Here's how you do it, come sleep — hatchet in one hand, knife in the other."

"That's right, and in this light, a person'll be able to see the claws rip your neck apart as that big bear lip trembles."

"Miles. Now I don't mean anything by it but, shut up."

"Look at the moon, will ya. She's lit up like an afternoon."

"That was some pork chop. My teeth are rate tired."

"I ate mine like a mitt. Was any of it even cooked? Listen!"

"What the fuck was that?" Looie's voice had dropped as in a well; his hand clutched the knife he ate with.

"Just the river."

"Yeah? Well, what about that! Let's get in the fucking tents!"

"You're right, the tents'll save us real well — Looie, it's not eight o'clock!" And then in the moonlight, silent as a doe on dew, out steps on a round river rock a red fox.

"Hello, Charlie."

"Don't tell me!" said Looie.

"Look at the tail."

"He followed us?" Looie rested his hand with the knife in it on the rock.

"Followed us? This thing lives here." I pulled a pork chop bone from the fire, cleaned it in the river and tossed it onto the hard sand. Charlie stepped for it, took it in his jaws, settled on his belly and kept a paw over his meal.

Neither of us slept. The river was like a Los Angeles freeway, sucking air from the cool gorge walls just above us. A bear could be at your tent-fly saying, "Eh, bais. Not much of escape route here?" My hatchet was at my hip.

It is that night when you think that you have not slept, that night when an event comes to wake you and let you know that, yes, in fact you have slept. The event on this night rivalled the rumble of a jet airplane stealing down through the gorge above where we slept.

I looked up at the blackness of the tent and as if he was at my ear I heard Looie holler: "Miles! Miles! What the fuck is that!"

Just then my tent was slammed with a wash to rock Noah's ark. I turned over and over in foam and only by sweet fortune had got my hand out the tent door. I gripped fabric as whirl over whirl tossed me head over heels. I drank a gallon but had enough sense to pull myself through, to kick myself free of the tent. *Bang, bang*, I rolled in a deluge of black, being struck and cut by sticks and logs and broken branches.

I got myself above water and saw a rushing white river stretch from bank to bank. Looie rode a bank of bubbles, stayed silent as he threw a big long arm at the surge then gave up fight to twist onto his back and be enveloped by the water. A pair of sams; I was flotsam, he was jetsam.

I kissed swell and spat spill, got my damn leg jammed and felt it come from my body. I looked to the shore; there was Charlie, watching, whimpering, looking about him for assistance. But another tide came and lifted what caught my leg and me up to mix us in the general disorder, my nose plugged with river wash, my molars crunching gravel as I sailed for a bend and was thrown, cut and torn, against an old dead windfall as half the river came down the nape of my neck.

My bones were intact. I climbed over the swords of branches of the old windfall to make shore where I heard thunder subside and the river settle like someone had turned off a faucet.

"Looie," I barked, sounding like that Hiroshima dog that had its voice box removed. Looie was riding and rolling the last of it. I got to my feet, he couldn't; he was tumbling again as if in the very last rolls of a car accident. Looie crawled on all fours, stood, fell like to kill himself. He sat, as a trickle of river bent to get around him.

My voice broke, "Get out!" I said. "She might come again!"

"Let her come. I survived that so won't ever die."

I helped him onto shore. We lay on the bank till the sun rose like a couple hobos beaten off the train and in need of a meal. Slowly bits and pieces of our gear appeared, caught on tree branches, between boulders. We gathered what we could. Looie found my glasses inside my destroyed tent.

"This makes it worse," said Looie. "They told us never camp in the rivers up here, these harbour rivers. The overflow of the hydro project of Wreck Cove comes down through them, the pent-up lakes of the highlands. Gates must have been opened last night and that's what smashed down the gorge over us. Why you and I aren't down with the eelgrass in the harbour as food for crab and starfish I'll never know. I'm gonna ask you once, Miles. Not a soul, tell about this."

On the way to the Cabot Trail, wet, groggy, cold, and broken, half our gear on our backs, we had to enter a Buddhist valley. Folks from Halifax owned the land, a hundred and ten acres. Their supreme leader of the universe had recently been here to feel the vibe and nominate this place as the greatest energy source in the history of infinity.

"What? The words of that don't even make sense," I said to Looie, who was telling me this.

"What I heard."

"I guess it's true, then."

Neither of us wanted to disturb any mediators, in wine or saffron robes, with shaved heads and carefree skin. "Man, you got to be some uptight to choose a life like that!" said Looie, a little bit too loud, his hair stuck up like an Iroquois brave, his face scraped as if from a fight with a lion.

He shivered openly as we came across a golden post stuck the ground, with Asian lettering on it.

We reached an old logging road used as a footpath. The sign here read: *Path of Light; First Field of Meditation.*

"Let's get to the river," said Looie. "I feel just like a conversation with people on a path of light after just swallowing the watershed for the Cape Breton Highlands. Maybe they got *a* light — and a smoke. I meet them in the park. Sour as old dishcloths. You just ruined their day, see. Tainted it, with your presence. People get possessive in woods. It's all theirs when they're travelling it alone. Anyone who comes across is a violation."

"What if she's nice-looking?"

"Whole different story."

We saw monks and got quiet. We waved.

We reached the highway where strung across a steel gate to the property was a limp festoon with faded Asian lettering.

"Nice size padlock!" said Looie. "Good old Cape Breton hospitality for ya, there! Welcome one and fucking all!" He was overjoyed to be free of the woods.

We hit the asphalt and began our "walk of shame," as he phrased it. Car horns bumped. "Ah, Jesus, I was afraid of this," he said. "That's failure, those horns, defeat, the bumping. They know who we are, probably me better than you. You're okay, you. Look at us. Couple of drowned rats, beat to pieces."

Someone hollered out a window, "Other side of the island's that way, bais!"

143

Looie muttered. Another car, a passenger pointed and the window came down, "Who's that wit cha, Miles? Up in the hydro dam, bais. Tryin to put the power out up there?"

They tooted horns, jiggled steering wheels.

Back in the house we hoped for heavy rain. Our faces searched the sea for patter. There needed to be something to explain why we were back. But this lovely flat balcony, lovely slim rails, nothing obstructing your view. "The woods, me son? The woods are horrendous!" said Looie. "Good thing I got a warden truck when I'm on patrol. And don't expect me to address any concerns down in a riverbed again."

Our legs were ruint from the up and the down of the hills, the lurching on that washboard carnival ride down the riverbed. Our arms were scratched from bushes, necks and ankles bitten from bugs, on foot, of wing; our faces, palms, shins and knees were beaten black and blue from climbing out of the flood.

"Rain, you bastard!" shouted Looie to the sky. Like Moses he struck a walking stick of Tim's on the balcony.

"They'll hear us across the water, Looie."

"It's my rain dance, Miles. I got to get her to pour."

A sprinkle of something cried upon the sea.

"I'll never live this down," said Looie, seated, pensive as a sage. "Nope. Park'll never let go of this one. That Fleur the coyote nut and her dog Allouette. She'll love hearing this. She was the one who made the remark to me. Oh my, camping in the river. But you got your promise, Miles. Yes, that Fleur knew I was going with the guy who knocked out the power to half of Cape Breton Island."

"Third."

"Mind if I say it was your boots?"

"It was my boots."

"Yes it was. The left and the right."

"Say it was my boots if it'll save your job."

"Part of me doesn't give a sweet old American you know what. Part of me wants to build a place over on the hill like you and say, 'Go to it, you bunch of fools!' Except there's this other one now."

He had his waterlogged phone in his hand, with a power cord to it. We looked at the sky. but our eyes strayed to my boots, paired at the entrance, their soaking wet leather had them appear brand spanking new.

"Go home!" said Looie. "A person could walk to Everest in those!"

A big rainbow appeared over the sea and rain fell through sun.

"In Japan, they call that the wedding of the fox," I said.

"Over here on the harbour I call it, 'I hope the sun will go bag its ugly head so a big huge thunderstorm can hit!' Last of the flask, Miles, drink it. We didn't even drink up there — how bad a trip was it! Ahem — Jesus, I just coughed up a trout!" A call came in on Looie's home phone, "Who, us? No, no. Yalp, yalp. Home, footwear issue. Had to make a decision on it, right one, I think. We're going again in September."

On my way to my cabin I looked for Charlie. I guess I will always look for him. I wondered if he made it back from the flood, if he got all the pork bones. I wanted him to see that I was upright. Something told me he knew. Looie's lady Fiona was at university the next province over. Looie had driven her up, making the fourteen-hour trip of highway construction, a couple of times. He couldn't be doing that too often, he said. He came to me one night and said his seasonal work was done. He wanted to give a winter-trial of a go with Fiona.

I remained in the cabin after he left. I needed to work up the energy to move back into the big house and it wasn't coming. Small spots, where I was, are so much easier on the heart.

It was those precious two weeks in late October when the leaves are roving Chinese operas, all bedazzle and bejewelled. I didn't have money to make it through winter but I learned from Looie not to bat an eye over the likes of that. "Everything but a hello from a stranger is ridiculous anyway," he remarked. "It either works itself out or it doesn't. And who taught me that?" I wonder if I talked like that when I was his age.

I didn't want to be in the Highlands tonight. It was winter in my heart and I could see my breath. I once knew the carnivals of Rio and the spice markets of Bangladesh. But a warm rainstorm hit and the beauty of the log cabin, with wind pounding a sound roof and rain gushing from fat sides, was such that I didn't want to sleep at all only to listen and stay comfortable under two sleeping bags.

On my last night in the cabin I got up to stir the fire and throw on a couple cancerous beech chunks and to close all out with one more stomp at Old Eleven, a hammering out of "Johnny Lillington".

> *My name is Johnny Lillington*
> *I'm from a Cape Breton coal-mining town*
> *I fell in love with a married girl*
> *Now my heart is forever bound.*

I Am Lonesome But I Ain't Blue

The deer are scarce this winter so I have little to say about that except that one night on the North Shore I saw two look down the ages of time. I had to stop the Rocket to take in better their stillness under soaked spruce. I will mention one thing, a dream. I curse under my breath when people tell me their dreams. It is a film plot in the ear, which should prompt any of us to take a hasty leave or pound the table for topic change. Here it is. A bear came down the mountain and into the house.

"You don't understand how hard it's been," he said. He had tired, watery eyes; dry, woods-smelling fur and said he was forty-one.

We were on the third floor, I plotted my escape route.

"We all end up hurting everyone. I've hurt so many, I cannot recall how or when or who anymore. I've lost my taste for food," he said, and looked at me and, with big bitchy instincts, backed up and growled.

"You see," he said. "There! There! See!"

I saw, all right.

"Because," he said, "I will now have to eat your stomach and you're not safe!"

I got on the other side of the door, holding the knob for dear life, barring that bear in the house. Sweating and trembling I got outside. He couldn't use the knobs. It was his state of mind, that was hair-raising.

147

It was seven in the morning just before Christmas and snow fell like cold ashes from Heaven. "Today's the day I'm heading her out, Miles," said my dear warden, standing with the slow snow gathered on his cap that read, Chip Factory. He had just finished cleaning his truck window.

"For good?"

"The winter, Miles. I only came this quick trip to get my rifles, see you. I'm leaving that bottled moose so you won't die, right away."

His tires crunched down over gravel and snow, his tailpipes smoked; alloy rims and big mud-flapped tires drove heavily out of sight. In late summer when he had crunched down over the gravel Looie had gotten two flat tires from the sharp stones I'd left in my lower roadwork. That big heart of his sent no blame my way; blame and blaspheme went to the manufacturers of automobile tires, to all rubber-makers in North America, Hong Kong, Japan, and Singapore. He and I went to the tire shop in Sydney and while there he expressed to staff his views on the tire world. Did he know the truth? Did he know the tire company had a sound product and that the stones of my driveway were the culprits? Stones, I imported? He denied himself my culpability, would not even entertain the thought of Miles or his road as being to blame. Is this a kindness that is common? Looie would never work for the national park again, he said, after getting in trouble for practice shooting. He'd hit something living.

I heard a tiny cough and throat clearing and looking past my frosty breath saw Charlie. He was sitting upright on his ledge, a white bank all around.

"Ho. Never thought I'd see you again."

I climbed up and he didn't scram. He sat regally on his ledge, merely twisting his head at my advance.

I crouched beside him. "What's wrong that you came back so tame?"

Blood was in the snow under him, I saw it deep in his paw prints. From where I was on the ledge I saw bloody prints trail to my door. He must have come during the night. His left hind leg was torn open, the paw caught in a length of brass wire that had a fir branch wrapped within it.

I got my coat around him and he let me take him.

I carried him inside the house and called Brazil. I knew a horse veterinarian. I had played music for their association. They once took me on a conference to South Africa.

"Is there any tear at the tendon? What a pity — poor Charlie."

"I can't say if there is. He won't stand. I don't want to make him."

"You will have to sterilize the site like I showed you with the horses. Remember the case of the wood splinter in the stallion's testicle? We got that one out. You held the horse so well. You must clean the wound as best you can, then, sew. That's all that is ever done in these cases."

"Sew?"

"With a needle, and thread. You sew pant cuffs. I saw you do it and cuffs are harder. Maybe use the fishing thread. Dip the needle in alcohol and hold it in a flame. You saw me. You will have to design a collar to prevent him from biting your work."

Someone was outside; I hung up the phone. Looie knocked lightly on the door and came in.

"Miles, you home, Miles? Jesus — you caught him!" Looie's black eyes burned a hole in Charlie and then in me. He was topped with joy.

"You caught him, Looie."

"What? Snare? Ah well, Jesus, I *am* gonna burn in hell." Looie had turned around on the road because he'd forgotten his Colt cigars.

"Hold him, Looie. I ain't taking him to any vet."

"Can't say as I blame ya. He's a fox — one. What you got is an escaped felon. Now you take it easy and don't you bite me, you little red fur walker." Looie got his jacket off to better close in on Charlie, who bit him on the fat part of the palm, the door-pounding part.

"Mother f . . . He drew blood! Blood, Miles! No, no — don't worry, Charlie? I'm okay, and I'll never set another snare long as I live. Except once more bite like that and I'm takin ya out back to the chopping block. Never heard of fox soup but I bet it's good. You guys are supposed to be smart — what're ya doing get caught in my trap? Another wives' tale, I suppose. Miles?"

"I'm busy, Looie. What?"

"She's pregnant."

"The fox?"

"Not the fox."

Looie was looking to the harbour north, his hands clutching Charlie's haunches.

"Looie? Fiona? Well, sir." I held my needle, drew two-pound fishing test through the eye.

"Well sir is right," he said.

"That why you came back for the cigars?"

"I needed a smoke. It is why I came back to Cape Breton, to get my head together."

"You never said a word."

Looie seemed like he needed arms to turn his shoulders to get himself back in the scene. He chomped on the plastic filter of a cigar as he gripped furry haunches. I had taped together the front paws before he came but Looie was nervous as an alley cat, saying his legs were growing weak at the thought of a needle passing through fox skin.

"Gave up smoking after that last beer last night," he said. "Today's a new day. I'll chew them, that's just as good. No it ain't. Ah! He bit me again! Nice gouge! I'll need the surgery! Ah — again! Miles, this is turning into a bear maul!"

"Hold him, Looie, I said hold him, please!"

There was the click of flint and I smelled cigar smoke.

"Looie? Ya got to hold him. Keep your arms in closer, I need him closer."

"Any closer, Miles, and I'll be wearing him to a charity. I'm just trying not ta get eat. How light are they, though. Except this one's got the fight of a Puerto Rican Lightweight. I was just going to say how I miss down here — ah!"

I spoiled three expensive razors shaving the site. By pinching the skin I got the needle to go in and the stitches came tight in around the paw. I knew how to tie a knot from mackerel fishing. Using a utility knife, breaking expensive blades, I lopped off the top of a pink road-pylon that the Tree Ghost kids were playing with. We got the pylon over his neck and then it was the pricey Home Hardware Tuck Tape designed for sealing vapour barrier. The pylon was secure; he couldn't bite the stiches.

"Would have been good to get that on prior to the operation," said Looie. "I'm gouged like sea plankton. Here, sew me up."

We studied him; it worked. A vet would have been a good profession for me.

"We done?" said Looie. "'Cause I like being on hand for an animal operation like I do for a mortician reassembling train crash victims for identification. Let me use the bathroom, to shoot some heroin for the post traumatic syndrome, then I'm blasting off."

"Night's coming on, Looie."

"Night! Miles, she's nine o'clock in the morning!"

"But look how dark it's getting. A huge blizzard's forecast."

"Which means I gotta get on the road, rate away!"

"You won't make it off the island when the world turns into a big whiteout. I'm from here. You'll be stuck outside a garage in Antigonish, overnight in your truck, listening to As It Happens on CBC. Looie? Tonight, stay. Tackle the drive in the morning. She can wait." I had made a mistake before. People could stay here now. Together, the two of them looked out the window.

"Let me call the other one, then," said Looie.

A big blizzard hit and at midnight Looie's girl Fiona had her baby. I was surprised. I thought he meant that she had only just got pregnant. She went early, though. Something had gone wrong and she was rushed in. The baby was being given oxygen and fed through the navel. I sat up with Looie and in the late hour, in the company of a raging winter storm, at the sucks and draws of the woodstove, I saw big Looie frown and his mouth go tight. We don't age in years, we age in nights. That Labrador mountain held his head in his hands in the purple chair that Tim had sat in. I said, "Loo? Loo? Come on, now. You're broke up like a Chinese mahjong set. They said both were healthy. It's a baby, man."

If you painted his face you would have made a couple million dollars.

"A baby?" he said.

"Yeah?"

"I don't get to live like you, though."

"Like me? Who the hell wants to live like me? I don't want to live like me. No one gets to live like the next person, Looie. You're the one with the good things happening."

Tears big as raindrops from an eave fell onto his new whiskers. I asked three or four times why he was crying. "I ain't tough as everyone thinks. Everything tears me rate to pieces. I can't watch a movie trailer."

"Ah, it's that way for everyone."

"Not for you. You're like an empty beer bottle in a summer ditch."

"An empty beer bottle . . . "

"Well. Up here all the time. Talking to the animals. Seems awful good to me. And why? 'Cause I'm fucked is why. You don't know what that is, Miles, to be stuck. I mean . . . Well . . . "

Looie had his burning eyes on me and I could not look away so well. Oh, the procedure in listening. I had been doing well with eye contact. With Looie, that is.

"Only feels that way. This is a good thing." I said.

"It feels that way because it is that way! Ah my, fuck it. You're right. What did you say that Odysseus once said, 'You get tired of mourning.' She's right. Except I'm tired of afternoon. Ah, let her all come if she's coming. Got anything to drink?"

"Just what you left me."

In the morning, a composed and hungover Looie laughed and said, "We're calling the baby Charlene after Charlie. The missus was dead-set against it till I told her the baby was a result of the upstairs here. Premature but the doctors are positive. This, Miles, is the best point in my life. I know how it all works. Everyone gets beat to pieces by life. I had at least this time on the hill. All started for me here. I'm not even going to curse anymore. Well . . . What was it your grandmother used for bad words, 'Landsakes'?"

"You tried that."

"Landsakes — did I? You're right, sounds like . . . well, never mind. I'll use 'cluck'."

He got his truck scrapped off and the motor ran.

He came in and looked at me wide-eyed as if his report card was behind his back and he had at last passed a subject. But he said nothing. In the back porch he stood, hand on the door, looking out at Charlie's ledge. He looked back at Charlie who lay curled in the purple chair by the fire. The Labrador peak then said in a high-pitched voice, 'Don't let the doorknob take you in the hole on the way out the door!' We say that when someone won't leave when they all set to go. All's different out that door, Miles."

"Get the hell out of here."

"You're here on your own. Why don't you get someone? Why didn't you ever get anyone? You're skinny but not too bad-looking a fella. You made it awful nice up here and you're gentle as one of those big puffy snowflakes fallin outside. Don't matter that the sun doesn't shine over here except for two or three months a year, some woman'll go for it. Because what's more overrated than the sun? Sun, me son? Sun's the thing to drive a person battier than I don't know what! You know that — those countries you were in. 'I have to go here, the sun is shining! I have to go there, the sun is shining! Run, run, quick! Better not miss the sun!' Holy cluck! Cluck? I'm not gonna say that."

"Get out of here."

"I better, 'fore I start makin even less sense. See, told ya — changed. Ah, you'll be all right here. I'm not going to worry about you. You got your little friend. Goodbye, Charlie. Sorry I almost ended your little red fox days but you left me with some pretty good scars. Sorry I near separated your hind leg from the rest of ya but I got your bites to carry with me.

Yeah, you watch — I'll be wearing glasses before you know it too, Miles."

I had to manhandle him.

Looie left under a moment of blue sky, but way up over the mountain. He 4x4ed it, angled his rig straight down the hill, gave it to her; went bucking, lurching, and plowing through three feet of snow before bursting through the big snowplow bank and onto the Cabot Trail. He fishtailed and was gone. When the big yellow plow came with its chains a few minutes later, its thunderous load buried Looie's tracks.

I was sentenced to a life of snow and wind and darkness till spring, but also stars and moon and animal tracks and the black-capped chickadees who winter here. And, crows.

But salt spat from the plow's tail, and from atop the highway monster came a warning orange, a slow circling light, circling, circling, touching a dark mountain in daylight, throwing tint out on the white and grey of a harbour ice. A crow cawed. A crow flew.

It wasn't night, just dark as the mountain stays through the day here in winter, and so in homage to light I grabbed Lucky Old Eleven and sang "I Am Lonesome But I Ain't Blue".

> *I am lonesome*
> *But I'm no fool*
> *We tried doing all*
> *They wanted us to*
> *Sometimes people*
> *Just don't get along*
> *And the best choice*
> *Is moving along.*

I Got the House You Got the Home

There was an ant war on the Cape Smokey stone. I had set slate grey gravel between this stone, gravel I carried in buckets from the shore. Memory of the boatshed loomed over me during my filling of the bucket. Memory of my carrying the chainsaw down and pulling the cord, walking inside and cutting down the crossbeam. The removal of the crossbeam would undermine the structure, have it fall and wash out to sea. But then I got a taste for eradication. Yes, at first, to have it fall, and a storm catty it out to sea, I would have burnt it had I not had enough dealings with police, fire, and Nova Scotia power people.

The red ant fought the larger black carpenter. On June 21st of every year the carpenter climbed an inside wall in a black-curtain mass. It was mating time and wings grew on male and female. If you were not careful they would enter your mouth. Before the wings came, I had followed their trail to a stump above Charlie's ledge. There I sprinkled gas. I watched how they stopped at the barrier, rerouted to continue on their path toward the eating my house. In the woods by the cabin these ants had munched a dead sixty-foot black spruce for a year. I cut the tree down and moved its logs down into the lower field, into harsh sunlight. It did no good. I could hear them when I slept, hear them in winter. This was in my house. I hoped for the victory to be that of the red.

Morning sun shone and I saw how they fought, bodies bent backward on rock and gravel, silence all around. The red were

156

a gang-up type. Two grappled with a carpenter on a tuft of sod when the party fell what proportionally could be a hundred feet, to resume death grips. I let my periphery vision take in the field of war. It was on the forest bank, in grass, on deck posts. There were heroes and villains but no cowardice. Strewn bodies were dragged to memorials.

I snapped on the outdoor light; the battle raged at night. A week later no ant moved. In the sun on June 21st no black-curtain of black carpenter ants climbed the wall.

Looie was gone and I carried in a huge armload of wood — the lazy man's load, a load that is done in one shot because you are too lazy to carry a second.

Charlie looked up from where he lay curled up on his purple chair. From the open door a draft swept across the plank floor to chill him and the raw daylight had him squint.

"Gimme a chance," I said. "I'll close it."

The pylon cupped his head like an audio speaker.

"You a megaphone, Charlie — Charlie? Charlie?" He looked at me. "I don't talk to animals. Do I?"

He whined in his foxy way, a half-hearted throat-clearing that seemed new even to him, a sound he might not ever employ out in the wild. His fur was faded and I wondered how old he was. I tried to stay back from him because when I came near he shook like a leaf. He whimpered when he wanted something; I did my best to figure out what it was.

"Ever have a bath, fox? In warm water? Soap can't be a big den item." There was a plastic tub I had found big enough to wash a baby in. I had used it to check the wheelbarrow flat and to mix concrete for small jobs. I filled this with warm water and with Sunlight dish-soap got the bubbles going.

He stiffened when I reached for him and, with the pink pylon in the way, I could not see his eyes. But dried blood clung to his fur and in around the wound. A bath should help ward off infection. Who knows what he fought in this human habitat? I set him in the tub and he puffed up like a porcupine. I squirted Sunlight detergent on his fur and lathered him. He fought but I got the job done. I dried him, covered him in a towel, and set him back on three pillows in his purple chair. He got down from this, shook himself and settled by a secondary heat source, an electric heater blowing a summer warmth. As if enjoying a car ride by an open car window, his muzzle faced the force. But it was too hot perhaps because he got back on his purple chair and lay like the debauched, the whole day, getting sleepier and sleepier. Heat from the wood stove knocked him out. His life on four paws had been one long hustle and the drug of ease erased all this.

"You have that creepy sleepy sick look Fairy the moose had. You won't end up in any jaws, you think, so all concern is dead. Go ahead. Let it carry you."

I lifted him to the white sofa and positioned him in front of the fire better. He turned his face for pink flames past the dirty glass, his ears twitched at crackling; his eyes stayed on the distorted dance of the flames.

When I turned the lever on the woodstove door to add another stick, he stretched his neck.

"We got used to fire, didn't we? Years, it's taken me to learn how to dry wood. I haven't mastered it. You're no woodsman just because you grew up in the woods."

The telephone rang. It stopped and rang again: our code; it was Paddy.

"He there?" said Paddy.

"Right here."

"You gonna keep him?"

"For now."

"Keep the thing."

"You never know."

I looked at an empty sofa. In the porch, the door was open, from the armload of wood I had carried in.

"Damn!"

"What?"

"He's gone, I'll call ya back. No. Hang on."

I set down the receiver and outside I saw in the snow little bloodied tracks accompanied by the scraping of a pylon, all headed for the mountain. Cold cut through my shirt. I came back to the phone.

"Mess with nature, see what happens."

"He gone?" said Paddy.

"That moose on my conscience wasn't enough."

"He go up the mountain?"

"Yeah, I gotta get boots on and go after him. He won't live with that thing on his head."

"Call me when ya get back. But we're gettin' a storm, you know, hundred-mile-an-hour winds."

When I had gone for the wood, snow must have gotten jammed in the door and the wind had pulled it free. On the step, biting a mitt to get it on, the same wind tore the door from my hand. It was frosty as hell tonight, the second big storm of the season forecast on the radio. And it was hitting.

"Guess it's in you never to trust, Charlie. A problem we share perhaps."

I pulled at the stocking hat over my head. I had to get better prepared. In the porch, I cleaned my glasses of sleet then inserted drier felts in my boots. I shook a box of matches and put twenty or so in a plastic bag, ripping off part of the striker. Compass? Do I even own one? I looked for Tim's walking stick and said to hell with it. I got outside and dug a foot in the mountain but the big drift that had always kept me from wanting to go above presented a problem.

I got to his ledge and rested. Tim's stick leant against the back of the house, I returned for it.

It took thirty minutes to make it to the Tree Ghost, a journey of less than a minute the day the kids were all stung.

The woods turned dark. I saw the fir stumps capped with snow. I had cut these trees to build the log cabin. As a boy I had feared the chainsaw; I now loved the biting power in my hand. I had worked my way up to cutting on a ladder, hanging over spinning teeth, ripping tongues and grooves and corner joints often with the machine full bore and inches from my face. Concentration was key. My time away taught me concentration.

I sang into the woods. I didn't have Lucky Old Eleven but sang because maybe Charlie would respond, come out of the dark snow, and I could lure him back to the house. He would not die then, collared and lame. I sang "I Got the House You Got the Home".

> Guess you're doing fine out there
> You got some friends who really care
> Pretty clothes, fancy shoes
> Again the girl they once knew.

The Middle Eastern Bird

Why, why, why. I'll never know why, but it was the bleakest winter you ever wanted to know and sleet fell to slice you to ribbons as a white world out and below said more, more, fall some more.

Temperatures plummeted to end sleet and freeze all to iron; not knowing where they wanted to be, wild highland winds hit, rose, became skyscrapers, reached icy fingers up then fell like cut curtains to be confused once more at a harbour ice floor. Floe from the Arctic Circle, from horizon on in jammed itself to the Gut and it was from here a lone seal emerged, a lone fat black squirm from flipper through to tail. The seal eased onto harbour ice and beeline it for its death — for wintering village houses, for dogs that had barked six dark months for just this. The dogs arrived in welcome, spent days circling, running in and biting, retreating and panting, turning to make sure the others had seen what it had done. Padded paws left perimeter blood markings as on art paper a child might to delineate the strength of the sun. One owner called but tide had broken the shore ice; there was no way out to beat the dogs. On the second day the seal sat in a pan of blood the size of a living room; on the third it twisted yet to ward off fewer pranksters; on the fourth a lone dog antagonized it but less and less, as fun had died. The curtain closes, rises, descends; highland winds are not more as eagles, crows, and gulls fill bellies in sun.

It didn't work, singing to the blizzard of the mountain in hopes Charlie would appear. I pushed up a black mountain with a gale in my ear under whipped trees knocking and droning as snow bits sailed off in bluster. My face was freezing, my wrists tender.

"If a man's feet are warm the rest of him should be warm."

Jay Hardwell. The other imprisoned Canadian. Jay had come from Woodstock, New Brunswick and was badly divorced. He had come to see the historical sights of this old world region. He wished to rove where yaks and sheep and goats coloured the land, where big bad wolves waited on the steppes to spill the blood of their gentle neighbours.

"Any place is safe for travel," said Jay. "It's media that says different and who writes that?"

I had been teaching at a Canadian college in Qatar, a peninsula off Saudi Arabia that pushed out into the Persian Gulf. Discovery of oil and natural gas had made Qatar the richest place on Earth. Newfoundland had been invited to set up and run a technical college that would train people for work in the fuel industry. And money? We made it hand over fist, a hundred thousand dollars for teaching the verb "to be". So ask, Shakespeare, of "to be" or "not to be". For this loot, "to be" it is. Canadians, among the highest taxpayers in the world, allowed to keep all of the first eighty thousand and accommodations thrown in. I had just begun making a dent in the debt I had in Canada, the house I built but could never afford. For the first time in my life, money was in my pocket.

I was not unfamiliar with being locked up. While drunk in Buenos Aires I had embarrassed a girl I lived with and she locked me in a secure section of her house, before driving off for the weekend. I got out of the first cage only to discover the door to the street was bolted. Escape here meant surmounting a twelve-foot wall topped with barbed wire and razor blades, with chards of glass fixed skyward in concrete and all neatly packed under a thin alarm wire running the perimeter. I hollered for release for two nights. The Argentines might have found it funny. They were quiet about it; a foreigner can be a scary thing.

I was in my hotel room when a knock came to my door. My time of making the big bucks had turned me greedy and mean. I had refused to spend on a proper holiday so I went where none would. Also, a longtime girl had a go at my inattention. A heart is tempered glass. Tempered glass blows in breakage, pieces pop after the fact, like freezer ice tossed out in the sun. The poets are right: don't make your work the amassing of money. But yes, much of your TV news is Big Brother hype, as I might have agreed with Jay Hardwell. I would not agree with him now, not with two turbaned men smelling of herds and pasture in my room. I spoke bits of the local language; I could nod, smile; I wore a black beard, had black eyes and was so road-careful after a life on it, remaining calm was not an issue.

"Your paper, please," said the taller, while the other set out to survey the room, touch a long spout from a tea set on the table, wink largely at me but his ease was no ruse. The taller was slim and skittish and had such a wolfish aspect, with his green-grey sharpshooter eyes on my passport, with his neat muzzle and even-cut silver beard grimacing, it was hard not to watch him. At his hip a leather belt showed homemade holes but something strained that belt. I saw his partner had only appeared shorter. The man was a hauncher. He presently stood militant; his shoulders back and ready. Stains were on his leather shoes to suggest he had once stood near drippings.

Separating my entry-visa from my passport, the Wolf inserted my passport into his tunic. And from his folds here he removed an oily gun. He pinched the visa. "I do not see your letter of invitation?" He pointed the gun at my violin, "And this?"

I felt relief — I was sure I could play my way out of this but when I went to elaborate he had given up on the violin and pointed to my clothing.

I was in tunic. I had bought it at a shop one street over because I had been stared at in my jeans and T-shirt. I was never one to take eye contact, long before any of this.

"Feels good," I said, a hand lifting the tunic.

His eyes stayed on mine and judge and gavel were in them. He waved his gun at the violin case and I was glad to return to this topic. Music had worked for me since arriving on the first tarmac of Singapore when I was twenty-one. But knew it was a problem for these people.

He made a motion for his friend to open the case and his friend did so at once, touching a filthy manicured finger to the A, making it ring. He clipped all shut and put the case under his arm while the A still rang, in my ear at least, the key for funerals.

The Wolf rubbed two fingers and a thumb but not as to indicate the universal money gesture, it seemed. I never learned what it was to indicate but, shame was in it. This was my father's violin. I had played it every day since my mother's death. I had never let it out of my sight, which is why it was here. I knew I would lose it one day.

With hands up I said, "I will come but this, with me." With my chin I indicated the violin.

"This is all yours," the Wolf said. "The clothing is ours." The only meaning I could ever piece together here was that my music represented beguilement and treachery whereas his clothing stood for modesty. He knew what the instrument meant to me.

They had me wear a burqa and marched me by gunpoint to a bullet-sprayed Toyota 4x4. They drove me into the hills and I saw yaks, goats and sheep then fewer and fewer and finally no settlement. At sunset we came to a checkpoint atop a plateau. This was the corridor. We rode the plateau to where land rose again but we did not ascend.

They placed me in a concrete building, in a room with a squat toilet, mat, bum-wash hose and a window of one-way glass on to steppes north, a barred window. Leaving the airport in Guarulhos, Sao Paulo I had seen prisoners hold bars like these as they let bare legs hang in the sun.

My captors brought cartilage on mutton bones, salty tea, potatoes, and maybe the fat of sheep. I could never be sure of what was in the gruel but the nose suggests for you too well of what some food may contain. I refused the meat, when I could. And then I got no more. Diarrhea was constant. Bumps of a rash climbed my back and the infection between my toes appeared on my forehead. It is better to stay dirty. You're avoided.

They had left me to my thoughts, to no set schedule as to when the food would arrive. I was in a cell the size of a very poor man's bedroom. At first, days just did not end. But then weeks passed and a month went by and time turned into that prairie road you're hitchhiking on with unwashed hair and whiskers and no one will pick you up. But day, week, minute, hour — those allocations of time ended. Not, seconds. Seconds came in which you studied every indenture in the wall, in the floor, the ceiling, the window, the door, the toilet contours.

Your thoughts got stuck in feedback loops: 'Where's the food? What have I done not to get it? Will it come again? I'm hungry. Where's the food? What have I done not to get it? Will it come again? I'm hungry.' For hours on end, these same five thoughts. Weather stayed foul and freezing, the sky outside the glass remained an iron grey and my bones stored up all the humidity of the freezing room. Snow was on a mountain and, though white and cold as it appeared be, it registered as a type never being knowable by me.

I slept on the mat and covered myself with a rat-eaten burqa, nibblings I could put fists through.

One night I came to the window as they were calling from outside. At night they say you can see through one-way glass so they might have seen me watching. A bonfire burned and around it they stood with glasses of tea and long-spouted teapots, each man free of his machine gun. One produced a bag and from this bag came my violin case, which they tossed on the fire. They could see me; they saluted me like American GIs. They slaughtered a goat and black sand drank blood against a night backdrop that reached into a hole of the world.

No one knew where I was. Ha! At the Newfoundland college? Are you kidding? Disappearance was the order of the day, the absolute norm in this cowboy world of the English teacher abroad. Because true pirates, those who travel anywhere for money and for a chance to be seen as exotic in some foolish race's eye, owe no goodbyes or farewells. They board for the next port of call. I had been travelling these twenty-five years, each new land had their white pirates and they looked just like me. But the ones I speak of came not as the traveller who desires the passport stamp but as the traveller who needs fare onward or, as in my case, maybe just to get home. People had given up tracking my whereabouts a long, long while back.

The Wolf asked for telephone numbers, for email addresses and street addresses. I was a commodity, but also the wrong Canadian to have kidnapped. They searched me online. But in this proud age of the mobile phone, with its one hundred and fifty contacts, ready and waiting for you, my name turned up zilch. I had a college phone but they left this region out. It was Canada they worked on. They did have me transfer all my funds online, sixty-one thousand dollars' worth, every dime of the only money I ever had. That should have paid my board. The only number I knew was from the old house of my childhood, the phone with the extra-long extension cord that reached into the Cold Room. But this is not true, and I don't need to lie anymore — I knew numbers. I knew my sister Marie's, for instance, but these guys wouldn't be frightening my family. Which, I realized, was all I had — family assigned at birth and none of my own making. It reduces you, when you realize how you have been successful in forging your isolation. Solitary confinement? It was a natural conclusion.

I heard the call to prayer in the mountains. I also heard the cooing of a mourning dove. But wind sang off the steppes at night. No computer, no phone, book, TV, radio; no pen. Nothing except the things I had done, had undone, and not yet done. I ate a dried curd called Kurut, goat milk was boiled to a paste; gummy rice came. But wind sang and sang and so I sang. I wrote lyrics in my head about spots in my village. I forgot them but more came. I forgot these too but form develops after a while, words soon last as they work in melodies. It was the one thing to kill the feedback loops. So careful you have to be with your mind.

I talk of food; it was the only event of the day. It came in the same blue speckled enamel bowl, a surface I had seen in broken cookware as a kid, in tin-can and diaper dumps that everyone had in the woods next to their houses before regional waste removal. I kept the squat toilet clean with the bum-wash spray, from which I drank. Night brought sleep out there to the mountains. But then maybe not, because the cropping and detritus would sing. One night I caught myself counting stars and touching my face, to feel either my fingers or the skin of my face. The Three Marys I saw. I had learned this constellation crossing into Paraguay for the casinos and the black-eyed ladies. I could never be sure whether I saw the Big Dipper here or the North Star that shot off its handle.

Coaxing myself to eat naan with poppy and nigella seed one day, while watching an actual wolf on the steppes, I heard them bring someone in. I had knowledge of a hall out there but not of another room yet they did not bring him to mine. "Contact the Canadian Embassy!" said an exuberant voice. "I'm a tourist!" Jay Hardwell, of Woodstock.

He said after a while, "Is someone here?"

"I am."

"Who's I am?"

"Miles MacPherson."

"Miles, eh? Me too, from my home. These guys the big T?"

"Or another letter."

"Yes."

"Jesus. That's it then, I knew I'd be tripped up one day. How long they had you, Miles?"

"I don't know. Ninety-one days."

"Jesus Christ."

"Don't eat the meat."

"Why? Sick?"

"Eat it then. They got mines up to the mountains."

"How do you know, Miles?"

"I saw a billy goat crack up."

I don't know if he saw the snow-capped mountains north. I don't know what Jay saw. We never talked about it. He didn't seem a Maritimer but what would I know? I've been out here.

It's too bad Jay was a doppelganger, for he too in this grand age of one thousand digital friends had no names for them. Like me he had no social capital. They went hard on him for that, harder than they did on me. I believe our estrangement puzzled them.

Light had become autumnal when the mourning dove appeared. He was getting cold perhaps and the nook of my glass afforded lee. A pink was on his head and a reflecting grey on his body. When you saw him in sunlight, from a certain point, dots appeared on the nape of his neck. I had been singing and he had to investigate. The one-way glass did not allow him to see who or what sang, though of what a bird's eye could see I can't be sure. He may have been able to spot my outline because when I shifted it rattled him. I do know I was able to walk right up to the glass and he didn't fly. Much of the time he sat in profile, detecting motion at the glass perhaps. He'd relax when I sang; he never left when I sang just dropped his head and cooed along as if the two of us were in a school play. I kept this going long as I could.

"They opened a door and I saw," said Jay, coming from questioning. "It was a dirty glass cabinet with a hookah and hoses inside, and a violin. I'm sure. Wrapped, though, in duct tape."

"How do you know it was a violin?"

"The shape. As a kid I got a hockey stick one year, wrapped in Christmas paper."

The next time they took him there was shouting and two rapid shots. I heard shovels that afternoon and, in the night, the close howling of wolves. I caught a glimpse of one slinking away with something.

The mourning dove liked morning visits. I don't know what species he was. I named him Spotty after the spots on his neck. I had recently stopped singing but Spotty would coo, would try to see in past the dark glass, "Where's my part of the bargain?" he seemed to say. The ones to coo are males — this was my recollection, in any case. "Okay, bird." I sang and he cooed. These visits were stop-offs, till the desert warmed most likely. "Spotty? Something remind you of your home in here?" The guards heard me sing. They brought me a book and told me to wash first. I hadn't been. You're let be when you're dirty. But I have said that and those are the loops.

On December 1st of 2008, after 199 days of solitary confinement, I heard *clop, clop, clop*. A helicopter was landing. My door came open and the Wolf stood in raw daylight, greyer, sadder.

"Song man? We will let you go."

He assisted me to the helicopter where a Western co-pilot in Ray-Bans strapped me in. After the clips were done and checked, he squeezed my upper arm and held it. This contact froze me like ice. I turned for the Wolf. It took a few moments to produce the words, "Do you forget something?"

The head pilot, in radio contact, made no move. He stared straight ahead.

"I do."

The Wolf returned, handed me a canvas bag with the instrument and bow inside, wrapped, duct taped, a fine dirt on the seams.

"I will never hear you play," he said.

"But you have."

He released me from damp green-grey eyes and we lifted off. The co-pilot set sunglasses on my face. I could only speculate as to why the violin had been taped. It was hidden in the ground but had he chosen the duct tape to allow it to breathe? Bow hair disintegrated in my fingers.

Fighter planes escorted us to Qatar and from there I flew seventeen hours to Montreal. There were cameras in the airport, the big eyes of their lenses. Stéphane Dion stepped from a crowd, in blue tie and wearing Old Spice. Eye contact meant physical pain. I recoiled at his touch. I tried not to look at the clocks on the wall and I could think words; I could not say them. I wore no long beard, no long hair, as in First Class they had given me scissors and a bowl. I was skinny. A French doctor checked me over and said I needed glasses, that I might have a touch of TB. There were three days of questions with senior Canadian military. They were writing a report on the other captive I knew. On the third day a pair of Americans arrived. One did the speaking.

"What exactly were you doing over there?"

"I was working. I was travelling."

"Do you know the United States of America is at war? That our ally Canada is at war? Mr. MacPherson? Where have you been these years? These countries you have spent half your life in? You're not married, there's no kids, no attachments. Someone like you would be an excellent candidate for sharing intelligence. Can you account for that? For this life you have?"

"I went for work."

"Are you a resident of Canada?"

"Yes."

"And what intelligence did you share?"

"Only what there is. None."

It was his experience, possibly, but he knew there would be no more from me. You can only ask so much of some people. I took a train to Truro and met my sister Marie.

Years advance and sisters become mothers. Marie was slow and careful with me but there would have been ease anyway; we shared the language of family and region, of memory, and age now. Marie could see through to me though, and damn these tears that would well and roll over my lip; it was like trying to stop the blood of shaving cuts. Marie and her husband Brian took me to the foot of my driveway.

"You built that big house up there," Brian said. "But no one can get up. Fix your road, Miles, so people can get up." I told them I didn't need one thing. I nodded and said yes to their questions, and nodded to their little car with smoking pipes as it drove off.

I climbed the hill to know again the sweetened air. I saw ruts of rainstorms and downed leaves in the dead grass. December. No snow. My violin and bow in the canvas bag the Wolf had given me. Light groceries were in a second bag I carried.

That first night was cold, as any house needs days of warming. Large snowflakes sailed past the window for bare ground. I dug out a little guitar my father had got for me in a flea market. A poor-burning fire was on and I had eaten all the sandwiches and burnt all the packaging. I tuned the strings and the little guitar buzzed all over the place. I coaxed my fingers to do just one verse of "The Middle Eastern Bird".

> *There's a Middle Eastern bird at my window*
> *I can see him through the one-way glass*
> *Oh, there's a party on in here*
> *He can't see but he can hear*
> *And for him to join in*
> *You don't have to ask.*

High on a Hill

I rubbed my eyes on the north balcony one summer morning
and saw a ring-necked pheasant. There came a flutter and a
burst in short flight. I saw a whirl of combed feathers and the
strut of a vanity-stricken chicken. Tints of brown, brass, and
sarsaparilla appeared on a body punctuated with tail feathers,
long and rigid. It led half a dozen little ones across the bad turn
of the Cabot Trail. I waited for the mishap but the hour was
so early, at leisure they crossed. They disappeared down over
the bank below the birches and I never told anyone about this.
There were many things I never told anyone about because of
how they would sound. I never saw a ring-necked again. The
pheasant holds mystery for me and promises that strangeness is
never far. I remember it now at the base of this big poplar where
snow covered my thighs and creaking winter branches looked
down on a lone man whipped by the wind.

I was in a hollow. The storm raged high in the trees but a
moon was out up there so visibility had returned. The lay of
the land was so much steeper on this side of the harbour, there
was more hardwood and it was not free from the village lights
below.

I left the hollow and followed Charlie's bloody tracks and his
dragging of the pylon. I met a tree ghost, one I had forgotten I
made. Dark winter crept out its face, a face waiting in the raw
cold of night. I brushed snow from his top when a big snowflake

landed on my nose. But what's this? I wore no glasses? I checked my right pocket, my left — and there they were, thank God. I got them on just as a snow shower from a limb pelted my face. What's the date? It can't be Christmas, but it is, thereabouts. Tim and I would make a fire in these woods on Christmas Eve down on the Plateau; we'd present each other little mickeys of rum and vodka. And in no time we'd be drunk and happy. But repair is here in these woods and I should be up here more no matter what the day, what the night, or the season. Darkness comes now like you would not believe.

I moved on, Tim's stick assisting.

That fox must have a den in the scree because the tracks were taking me there. Yes, the scree, the tracks end here. I looked high above and remembered seeing this from the other mountain when I was a kid. Overhead was little cloud traffic but a fierce wind suddenly rushed the little traffic straight across town. It must be the eye of the storm, as they say. The moon gives the visibility of a day with an eclipse. But what's that? My name called?

"Up here!" I hollered back, then regretted it because you can't trust just everyone with this fox situation. I shouldn't have interfered with the animal. But who would be trying these woods on a Christmas night, the darkest time of year? It's the play of the wind. The old guys would. The old guys don't come up here anymore; they're too old and if they did they would never sound out. It wasn't me, I'm not wanted; I'm in hardly anyone's life. Maybe it's a car accident down on the Cabot Trail. Ah, my — make this quick.

I placed a foot on the snowy scree, on a large boulder and I surveyed the playing field. Old Man's Beard hung on bordering spruce. It seemed ready to drop yet probably had sat there since before the ice age. Snow came in at my throat from gusts carrying it out of the trees. There came the blow of snow with a granular texture and I lost sight of my tracks. I had set my stick against a tree to adjust the tongue of a boot. Dark spots rising and zigging above me were his blood. His hole looked to be top centre but I will slip and break a leg if I attempt this. This particular scree was made up of boulders the size of cars. If I took the sides I would lose his tracks. There's hopping from one to another if I have to. I had the moon for visibility but I knew these storms and I would not have it for long.

But there? Hello? It was the prettiest northern pelt. A pelt with breast forward, forward and stout. It was no fox. It was the northern coyote in its boreal habitat and as proud a creature as there ever was. What did that Park one say? That it came from Western Canada and picked up wolf parentage in Quebec. I was far from home. And where's my stick? Back against a tree at the bottom of the scree.

I made no eye contact with the coyote but turned for the far off, snow-capped White Hills, the highest point in Nova Scotia. Oh — I thought of the coyote and of all it represented; I thought of who and what I was and where I was. Would it be fooled by my casualness? Indifference does not live up here. It was then the flash of another pelt stirred up my breath real well. They was a duo of players, players that sniffed my fox's blood.

The woods appeared to watch as I wondered how the scene would play out. And in my casualness, my footing slipped and down my leg went singly to bone on rock, my body weight naturally countering. The crack reached my inner ear. The coyotes watched from snowy stones, comfortably watched the lowland fool learn law up here. Pristine and starved, they waited and watched, as such is a supreme hunting tactic.

I wrested my leg from the boulders. I bit off a mitt and, above my boot tongue, felt bone protrude under my long john. I had been a ski patrol; it was the fibula of the right, a compound fracture. Bone pierces skin and there is a risk of infection. I had been waiting for this to happen. My body had gone to pieces in that room overseas, though I had not written in these circumstances, of falling on a mountain. These massive rocks are ice covered; you cannot walk on them. I had a hunk of bread in my pocket to barter with, but I needed to make it to the trees, get upright, get the stick, and all I had was gravity. Then I saw the shadows.

A pack waited below black spruce. Brothers, sisters, cousins, and aunts in a shuffling I had heard in the lions abreast the African water buffalo, before a lioness would twist in grace to rip hide.

A bordering tree shook its load, as the higher coyote pair sniffed for age, gender, health. What they learned honed their hunger. The smaller blinked in a personal snow squall.

The stirring in the spruce made me think there was a dozen there, a rogue pack. The pack that had lured the dog across the ice? The pack from the night I had the gun?

I squinted toward their sparkling grey eyes. They were so light of foot; they had to be on snow crust. But why did they not charge? My easy motion, I thought. It was then the shaggy two above bayed with all that was in their ribcages. My urge to run despite the broken leg overpowered me but I stayed in one spot. They'd have to make the first move. The larger of the duo panted, paced, paced in a silver dark that showed the face I recalled from that night. Wind caressed the other's pelt. Below me the woods rustled with a community.

I tried; I could not walk. The cuffs of my pants had frozen black with blood; my boot leather looked waxed as if with motor oil. My eyes stung. A broken leg on a mountain in winter. My laces clicked.

I hoped the smaller feared the loud magic to end life up here, the gun. I hoped her fear would keep the larger back. I had a long way to go, to back up. I needed that stick. I found the smaller coyote's pretty eyes and peered into them.

A gust blew a crown of fir down the slope. I got this above my head to make myself giant. They were buying none of it. Hunger, see. It eats at the belly like a towel wrung in strong hands. To eat is not a question of desire. My blood was on the slope.

I felt for the matches; animals fear fire. But why did this seem the greatest of myths? Why did I see these northern animals enter an inferno to eat flesh? The larger leaned, readied like a plough then made for me. His mate pulled ahead by a stride. I waved my fir crown: "Haw! Haw!"

Suddenly a small creature was between. It dragged bandages, on its head a pylon. It barked and the pair dashed for him as he leapt down a hole, their jaws biting at air behind hind legs. The fox popped out of another hole and the coyotes went mad for him. I took two quick breaths and rolled to the treeline, near the dozen. I heard aching breath and hopscotching now.

Biting off both mitts, pulling Old Man's Beard from the crown, I eased out a match and striker paper. Fire flared in my hand. The pack sniffed sulfur, yelped, circled me. Tails whooshed, eyes sparkled, ears were trained back as if wet. Growling came from muzzles so sleek and sharp.

Smoke filled my nose and my hand was half aflame. I waited for a grey incisor to clap my wrist. The crown flamed and Old Man's Beard puffed like gasoline.

Upslope I saw the two dig, bury their snouts, their pelts wriggling for that fox. I set my fire down, broke off a dead branch, ten inches, dry and deadly.

A coyote came hard and I dug my wood in its side. I know I broke skin. Another charged and I gouged his face while another chewed where my leg was broke. Two screamed to leave the pack. My fire exhaled and died in an instant.

For a second time I heard my name as a coyote I worked on bit my jacket, another tore pants above the boot. But then teeth broke through my thigh and through my left hand.

I cried out, grabbed one of the bitches and jammed it onto the spiky dead branches of a spruce. Lips and gums were on my face, pinching and lifting, and I gritted my teeth as I felt my cheek go from my jaw. I took the smoking bush and embers and waved it, jabbed it, swung at fur and front legs flashing near my face where mechanical teeth maddenly bit air.

A gun sang and all ended. There was but a pup gnawing at my leg above the break. I punched this in the throat and saw cross-slope a man bent for aim. Muzzle fire lit an old determined face. Sammy.

Sammy shot again and shot again. He took what seemed two steps to me in a jacket too big for him and that smelled of stove oil.

"You're their meat! We're not out of this!"

I was hyperventilating and could not answer.

"Ya tore up bad? Jesus! They went for your face, they do that. Listen! Look! Not giving up! Haw, I said! Haw, fucking, haw! Take my arm, Miles. We have to get you up better so they can see you're up. They'll back off with the two of us, up." He pulled me with real strength. "I'll get us down out of this but we got a piece to go."

"They still here?"

"Catch your breath, catch your breath."

"I'm bleeding."

"You got to calm down. You're shook up, Miles."

"My leg's broke."

"Christ. Lean on me, I'll get us down, just keep off of my snowshoes. This's Christmas Eve, Miles. What are ya doin' up on the mountain? Here — I'll get off another round. There! You maligning fuckers! I wanted to raise my traps, this snow coming. You're lucky I was up here. Did you find him?"

"Who?"

"The fox? I saw the blood. How you were following him. I called out."

"He's hurt."

"Never mind about him. Take my arm and don't be shy about it. This your stick? Take it. We'll get down off this hill. They're drunk on blood, adrenalin, and starvation."

"I don't think they got him."

"Who? Jesus, it's black. Come in the moonlight."

Long white hair hung from his head. He looked like an old frosty man who never dies.

"What?" I said, when he grimaced at seeing me.

"They opened your face. You're bleeding all over the place and they might have torn an ear."

"Away, away?" The knowledge almost made me black out.

"Nah, Jesus. You're good. Here, I'll ease your cap down."

"You see my glasses?"

"Your what! Miles, please no! You and your goddamn glasses, I heard all about that. You're lucky to have your life and you're still looking for your glasses. Listen, will ya, they're not giving up at all! We're not going back for glasses. They're following us. Wait. Here, bai, they're stuck in your collar, tangled, bent. They must have been on your face all along. Wait, I'll get them off ya. I got them. I'll put them in my pocket, see? I'm putting them in my pocket, that all right with you? I'm zippering you up. Just tugging here."

"Is that one?"

"It's something. Keep walking. Let me get this gun off my forearm. No, fox maybe. Something's caught around his head. Lots of things have dens up here in these rocks. It's what brings the pack."

"Can we go, Sammy?"

"We are, Miles. Hear the yelping? I never heard the likes, in close like that!"

"What's that there?"

"Bai, that's the Newfoundland ferry doing a crossin' in close because of the storm. She's lit like the Palace of Versailles."

"And that?"

"That? That's a goddamn moose is what! Is every Jesus thing on hoof and paw out up here tonight! But this hill was always bewitched according to the old folks. Two brothers were up here years back, and they got separated. I knew them. They spent the night and came back insane. That's how powerful the woods is. So march it, double-time it. Keep hopping like you're doing. I dropped my last bullet back there and I only might have one round left in the chamber. Hear, the snort?"

"I call him MacIntosh."

I was on Tim's stick, pain hot and complete like the front grates of a working woodstove on the whole day.

"I call him let's get the hell off this mountain and down into your house 'fore we're eat! Sweet Lord Jesus in Heaven! Don't put weight on it, Miles. Use the stick. Now, bai, you get yourself someone up here after this! You can't be up here alone!"

Sammy somehow got me down and his wife brought his truck. They rushed me to Neils Harbour Hospital. I got a tetanus and rabies shot, and I got cleaned up with alcohol and stitched. The leg was set then put in a cast. An American doctor on term did the work. Throughout he hinted at who I was. Sammy at last said it was not right for him to be asking me these questions.

Back home, Sammy sat with me after his wife, Clara, had gone home. He called her.

"Clara! Grab the grub and the grog and get it in the truck! Christmas's on Miles' hill tonight!"

Sammy unclasped fingers the size of hotdogs, where they were knit over his belly. He reached for my guitar, "I heard ya sing up here all them nights. This one I learned off ya, "High on a Hill". That how ya call it? Well, it applies to all us out on Smokey here:

> High on a hill we're all high on a hill
> Just take the path up to Cold Water Mountain
> There's a magical fountain
> That really likes counting
> Just ask the water what comes after one
> And you'll hear the water say,
> "Yalp — have a good one!"

Night Has Come

Rain poured from the heavens outside Cape Town. Table Mountain looked as if a dump of road salt topped it. I was with the Columbian, Argentine, and Brazilian veterinarians who were at an international conference. A call came in from the Stellenbosch region about an injured horse. Alexander and Alexandra, stallion and mare, best of friends had some trouble. The stallion had been fooling with Alexandra, chasing her, nipping her. And in a wet pasture Alexandra had kicked the stallion and broken its leg. Dutch owners called the university as their vet was travelling. Thais, from Columbia, volunteered to go.

Thais had the black ebullient hair promised on the back of shampoo bottles, a pair of deep-set, dark eyes that twinkled when she talked with her slight lisp. She was in love with Gilberto, my Sao Paulo friend who had arranged this very trip for me, possibly to pair her off with me. Thais' love for Gilberto had hurt so much she had to be hospitalized in South Africa. It was mostly vomiting and she recovered. I had asked her to help me with my Spanish.

"My English, Miles! It is important!"

She was considering kissing a man, she confided, to break the spell of Gilberto.

"Could that man be me?"

She laughed and laughed. "English, Miles! Please! It is important!" Her eyes burned several holes in me, clouds parted, trumpets sang. "But who knows," she said. She nodded and went seriously off with her horse bag. A woman like this, dying of love?

But the rain, the rain, the rain. Thais assessed the situation then called her colleagues in Cape Town. We could bring the horse into the university and as a team they would try to mend the leg. It was risky; a horse is a delicate creature, with its precise diet, its rapid decline when things go wrong. This is what Thais was communicating to me. We got a truck backed up to the paddy; the angle was bad. The mare Alexandra waited a little way off. Local winery workers stood soaked in the rain. The Dutch owners and their daughter could not watch but could hear as Alexander slipped on the gangway, falling heavily into the back of the vehicle. It thrashed for a full minute and Thais, inside, barely managed to escape. She got kicked in the head and there was bleeding. She cried like the owners. The horse was lying on its side with its femur broken, its lower leg snapped fully. Thais spoke to the owners in a cabin with an un-shaded light bulb. The daughter ran to the main house and the family followed. Thais had neither barbiturates nor license to administer a lethal dose here. And the university was too far. They shot the horse and the workers brought a tractor. They buried Alexander at the end of the soccer field.

But someone was climbing the high-bank path up to the house, a man with trimmed beard and gapped teeth visible when he stopped to rest. He carried no clipboard, wore not the government jacket of the meter reader — the only other to attempt a climb in the deep dead of winter. I had carved a warren in the snow up and around to the back door, which is where the man stood suddenly, catching his breath.

"Give me a moment," he said. "I have one foot in Nepal. The other in Tibet. Holy mother. Francis Pine. How are you, Miles?"

I'm not good, having a stranger arrive in winter. I wanted the business first before I offered tea.

We went in.

"Is that coffee I smell? I drink half-cups. Black, if you're offering. Oh, I have to take in this view. Will you look at that? I don't know what to say about it, but you look out on that, Miles? All day?" He had blue eyes and an accent, a mildly elbowing pattern found much south. He unzipped his jacket and raised a camera.

"Mind if I take your picture?"

"Please, no."

"They told me you were easy-going! Miles! All right, no pictures. Is that a journal? Wow, it's a big one. Handwritten."

"It's my father's."

"I met him in Halifax, Kenny. He was a veteran of the war. Okay. Okay. Miles. You have a story. We've been doing interest stories a long time in the region. People have to know what you were through."

"I don't want those animals harmed."

His eye contact came complete for this part of the conversation, "I didn't come for the animals."

"Well, I don't talk about that."

"But people got to know. I have been up here half a dozen times looking for you. I've called, written, emailed. You don't answer your phone. People have got to know!"

"Maybe, you have got to know. Maybe, you have got to go."

"I'm not up here to disturb anyone. But, one of our own was involved in this!"

I didn't know what *own* he meant but I said a few old world words then watched him walk down the hill. He fell. He rose to fall again. I watched his smoking tailpipe. This is a drop-in culture, yes. But the drop-in is a thing that ended for me.

The phone rang, in spring. It was my sister Marie.

"All right, who's dead?" I said.

"Milly Molly Meaney."

Damn it all. I looked across at the ottoman by the woodstove, at XXIX, *The Voyage of the Beagle* by Charles Darwin. How could she do that? She didn't give me time. I thought and thought how it would be great to meet her in the spring of some year and tell her how I had read it all. Five Feet. I never would have done it without the glasses, true — but it was her having had me carry that damn library out to the old Rocket, and making me promise to read them that set me on the journey.

"They want you to play." said Marie.

"I don't play, Marie."

"Think about it, Miles. You got to break back in."

Yalp, nice sight, me entering the church. Here he comes, "Kilometres! How ya doin', Kilometres?" No, I haven't been in the church since the priest accused me of breaking all the windows in the parish hall back in the seventies. That, I did not do.

I parked the Rocket in the new graveyard, a skip north over the old graveyard, which was alongside the church. With my violin I stopped at Tim's mini grave, moved soil, and brushed at the inscription. I replaced the soil and approached through the old graves. I saw here the hole and purple carpet, the brass rails with drops of dew. All was set to lower the casket by canvas strips. All was set for the little woman's bones. She got this, at the end of her life. It was one of the great achievements I had seen in this rickety world, a village showing respect for a member when so much out there was 'what can I get and for how little'? But that was here too.

At the rear of the outside of the church, down past the vestry, I saw the woman in the Cabot jacket. She was laying out her shovel and rake. She must be back on for the year, I thought. Great. Someone else to make me feel guilty. That's probably a good job. Her ride-on mower was in the dark shadows of a buttress north. I nodded, but turned attention to hole fifteen of the golf course, up past the old apple trees. Patches of snow were in the hollows of the sand trap. I moved my violin to the other hand and entered the church.

Ah, but what a little gang. And there was the casket, in the aisle, above the crucifix in the tile. She was too old for them to be crying their eyes out, but I heard a sniffle. And I felt good that it wasn't like many families who are all over the place with sorrow. But this is the start point for the war to begin over that property by the river.

There had to be half a dozen men up front, all of the same height and with red faces and bald heads. A couple of them had women, even well-behaved kids. I saw other women but I didn't know this gang at all and they could have been daughters or cousins. I did know, ah, what's his name? What's that guy's name — Adidas suit? It'll come.

No, but this would be some accomplishment if I could go out like this. Couple words at 10:00 AM on a spring morning, between the history of the world and a Tuesday, crows out past the stained glass, gulls in from the sea.

The caretaker with her Cabot jacket entered. She took her cap off, blessed herself, and sat at the very back of the church. Oh, I know this type of parishioner. But she must be obligated to come in and attend ceremonies, because she can't be having her ride-on going full bore and spinning around in smoke above the graves like a maniac trying to get her work done, not when something like this is on.

"Are you Miles?"

I turned and faced an elderly woman.

"I'm Mary, Miles. We went to school together. I married Neil Landry."

"Hi, Mary."

She's my age?

"I will be singing today so if you'll just play a couple bars, on my cue, at Communion that would be grand."

Grand.

"Mary?"

"Yes, Miles?"

"I don't believe I know what bars are."

"Measures, then."

"Oh. Where do you want me?"

"Anywhere, Miles."

"Can I go up in the balcony?"

"Ha! Still hiding from the gang are we, Miles? The balcony would be grand."

The creaking stairs let everyone know I was heading up, in avoidance of all, to hide from the gang. Well, they would need something to talk about after. But it was good up there and, when Communion came, I put that old violin on my shoulder and played "Coralee's Lament". It was a mistake; it was so damn sad. I didn't mean for it to go that way but they were all down there crying their eyes out and you can't speed up or throw in a positive flair when you've established a tone. Even the groundskeeper who, in the end, had come up behind the family for Communion, pinched at her nose. I had to look away. But wait! Am I beyond those bars and measures she told me about? Doesn't matter. I couldn't quit and that Mary one I was supposed to know wasn't looking up anyway. I brought it around to an A, drew the bow full for the end. It was a funeral. They've been known to be mournful. Oh well. More for them to talk about — "And he tried to kill us with some strange classical music he learned overseas in a monastery or something I think it was." Blame it on the old church and its balcony, the witnesses to all the christenings, weddings, and wakes here.

I went down fast to get the jump on everyone but those creaky steps slowed me and when I got to the bottom, the casket was going out the door. Now, I really have to follow.

We were outside. Rain had started. Gravel was underfoot. They were in city overcoats, slacks, shoes, neckties, dresses, and gloves. I was in my long wool coat, too big for me.

"How you doin', Miles?"

I looked and beside me was my old friend. How sad when he was forced to say, "It's Harrison, Miles."

"Good day, Harrison. How ya doin' old-timer? Where ya hangin' your hat these days, Harrison?"

"Up in Toronto. I have a construction business, believe it or not. I've been married twice and spend all my money paying for upkeep on divorces."

"I suppose."

"Back from overseas, eh, Miles?"

"Back, yalp."

"But you had trouble, too."

"Some, yalp."

"This's what's left of my family, Miles. We all pulled out. No, I heard all about ya. It was in the *Globe and Mail*."

"Oh, yeah."

"I'm glad you're home, bai. This might have been the place for every one of us. Still, that music near kilt the family."

"I didn't mean that."

"I know, bai. Was that your mother's tune?"

"How did you know that?"

"We're all gone, but we're still from here."

It would have been easy to mention the red books but that would bring it around to myself again, so we just walked on and talked about the golf course, an activity I'm sure neither of us pursued or thought about since our god-awful caddy days.

"Dear Friends," said the priest, and we bowed our heads. There were sniffles and a crow whooshed; kids looked at their parents. The priest dipped — I can't believe I know it — the aspergillum in holy water, in probably the same silver pail I held in the similar service of a priest, my little white gown over the robe of a hundred snap buttons. The priest left. I saw the workboot of the caretaker jam down on the back of a shovel.

On the walk to the car I saw the sons gather, the men. One reached in the trunk of a Monte Carlo. "Bais. She's not the place, but she's the time!" I saw Harrison wave off a drink. He waved to me as I got in the Rocket. I drove home, took off my dress shoes and pants and got in my jeans and Brazilian leather slippers. I got out the guitar at the kitchen table, near a red book open on page eight, XXII, The Odyssey by Homer. Well, halfway through, the Five Feet that is. And I read this one before I got into one for old Mrs. Meaney, "Night Has Come".

> Night has come
> And the dark is here
> I have my fire
> And my blanket near
> I don't have you
> To say good night to
> For we did part
> And all that's through.

The Twister

I can never get the partridge out of my head, the one I saw in the frozen apple tree in the silence of November. It was a time when any remaining leaf hung stiff as copper. The creature pecked at icy apples and I could hear its progress long before I could see it. It worked the morning and into the afternoon of a cast-iron cold day. I thought it would never leave. How easy it would be to shoot him, to pluck him from the dead ground and eat him with salt. Nature provides such creatures for when you cannot muster the strength of the big hunt. They are there for the taking, out in the open, the least defenseless of the scavengers. They are able to fly but a few yards and not at all fast. He was back the next morning tempting my hunger. Him, I let be.

Springtime saw my companions, the eagles, spin over the harbour. I was coming from the Cradle, walking with Tim's stick. I had paused on the Plateau, near the Tree Ghost, when I saw the pink pylon. There is no doubt it was the same I had affixed to Charlie's head; the expensive Tuck Tape was there. I had tried not to entertain so much thought as to what might have happened to Charlie. I figured the coyotes waited till he came from the scree and had eaten him. I imagined he waited in his hole, got stuck, and starved there. But we had seen him when Sammy was bringing me off the mountain. And Charlie had eaten from me that day so maybe he outlasted the hunger of the coyotes. The obstruction would have remained the challenge but it was before me on the bare ground, chewed off. His missus, perhaps? I stood above the house, above the ledge, the harbour in full view. I threw the pylon below to where I would pick it up later. Foxes do mate for life.

The eagles were in flight, Baby One and Baby Two. They did not have white crowns or white tail feathers, but immature dark feathers and therefore appeared huge. The white crown and tail of adulthood brings a shrink to appearance; soaring throws less of a shadow. But these might have been new offspring.

On the balcony east I played "Red-Headed Sylvia" on the harmonica. The eagles came to investigate so I named them Fidolin and Gaita: *harmonica*, in Spanish and in Portuguese. They left me. There was the feast of a washed-up walrus on late year drift ice down at the gut. The day before I had seen them hunt mice scurrying over snow still in the hollows. Late at night I had seen them up the North Shore, dine on a baby bear hit by a car. Fish was their preference, but ice was on the harbour yet.

It was spring and Fidolin and Gaita were busy growing. This brought me guilt. As, I was on my hill with my wheelbarrow cleaning winter refuse, sticks and leaves and run-off gravel; I had no job. Nothing did I produce for market nor did I hunt my food. A Scotiabank credit line was my walrus carcass.

Limping, I climbed to the log cabin then up to the loft. The day before I had seen where a squirrel had laid half a dozen babies up on the loft. Pink and purblind, each was the size of half a finger. The mother had eaten through my mohair blanket to get her incubator going. I threw the blanket back. Today I saw the six were gone. And this is where I was, my legs dangling from the loft when I looked through the little window to the brook that supplies the cabin.

Franklin waded out there, with his bent wing in the water. But something dangled from his beak. It could have been a worm except that it appeared to have weight to it and, it shone.

I approached the brook and he flew across the road. I wanted to holler to him, to ask him what he was doing over here and why he no longer said hello. But I thought someone was walking below so I kept quiet.

I stepped around the roots that clung to a mini ravine and came to emerald moss, puffed, soft and plentiful like a festival of toads. It was here the bird had dropped a copper wristband with an inscription: *Argyle Meaney, Tel: 902-285-2783, Diabetes.* And then I saw it — in a singular heap, Franklin's treasure trove.

It was under a bloom of moss. There was a hoard of shells and shiny beads, coloured bits of smooth ocean glass, a sewing needle, a miniature gold picture frame with a washed-out man and woman. There was fishing line with bobbers, ancient spinners, and tangled lures. I found marbles, maybe decades old, and even a spunky — which I pocketed. Roots held a gold earring that I could not quite get because they had grown through and around it.

But car tires were on the driveway. Someone was ripping up the latest sod that I'd had delivered by truck and carefully placed to line the tracks. I came down over the bank, slowing when I saw a woman, her arm in a rolled-up sleeve out her window, her hand clutching her door, her other hand rocking the wheel. The car was the identical model to the Rocket, a Ford GT. I looked up at mine to be sure.

"You should really consider fixing this driveway," came a raspy voice when the car stalled under the apple tree.

But the woman clutched it and braked it, twisted her ignition on and off, and got it going, gunned it. And I said nothing as I saw her completing the dashing apart of my work. She quieted, gave up, let the car roll back to below the apple tree. In thick mud it slid and she pulled up so hard on the emergency brake I thought the cable would snap. She opened her door, heavy with the vehicle sitting at forty-five. She eased out workboots, tapping heels, tapping on her rocker panel as if she was about to go on carpet. She got out with effort, stood, and straightened. She wore one of those light lumberjack jackets but she reached inside for a Cabot High jacket. Yes, the graveyard girl.

She put on the heavier jacket, quite possibly because her large breasts embarrassed her. She handed me her key and lifted her chin. "I won't even attempt it," she said.

I reversed the car off the slope, swung it into the built-up field, and pointed it for back across the harbour. Under the apple tree that tore the strip down Tim Dickey's truck she waited with an arm up against the trunk. "Ya leave any transmission in her?"

"Did I?" I said.

"She's slippin', the tranny. That's why I couldn't get up. Engine's gotta be warm." She took in the view, plucked a blade of winter grass, and chewed it. I passed the key by its singular red ribbon.

"Biggest kinda black crow flew off with me lunch," she said. "I let sail a leather workglove but missed. That wasn't enough. Another swooped and got hold of my medic alert bracelet. They were two-teaming it. I can't work with the thing on my wrist. But that's it, I said to myself, and hopped in the car and tore after the one with the bracelet. I trailed him all through Ingonish and he kept on up the Salt Lake till I saw him turn for here. I floored it past the bad turns at the ski hill and was almost kilt. He come this way? You see anything fly by with a bracelet?"

She swatted at a bee. "Jesus! The size of that! I heard there were bees over here! Must be after the apple blossoms." We looked at the blossoms, their scent dropping like a mist. "I'm just after starting work for the year," she said. "Mower's probably still running over there."

I passed the bracelet.

"Now ain't that something. He didn't have it long! Someone told me you taught a crow to speak, this the one?"

"Who told you that?"

"No one."

"That's him. But he came here saying hello."

"I always wondered what you had going on over here. Is it a monastery? I mean, you're in with the Buddhists, aren't ya? Up the valley? Those Halifax people? And you're a painter too or something, aren't ya?" Her thighs could haul a tractor out of a ditch and her nose was a flaked Christmas bulb but the prettiest grey eyes sparkled with an intelligence, an intelligence that stayed too well on the subject. Many of the best of sharp-shooters supposedly have grey eyes.

"I have a notion," she said.

"What's that?"

"Ah, you don't want to hear it."

I closed my eyes, "What's your notion?"

"To ask you out."

"Oh."

"Why not? Why the hell not? What's wrong with that? You can't be living over here like this. This ain't the Iron Age, me son! I mean, there's a whole world's down your driveway there. I heard all about you falling off the mountain and getting your face all beat up. It doesn't look so bad. You were supposed to break all your fingers and the Department of Lands and Forests rescued you in a gurney. A bear maul, was it? You can't trust them black bears. Listen, six o'clock, tomorrow, I'll be by. I'm Argyle, you're Miles. I was younger than you and you don't remember me but that's all right. We'll go ta get a bite ta eat in Sydney, watch a movie, head her home before midnight. That sound good? You can't go on living like this, a community's here. So I'll drop by, so you be ready. I don't need a number or anything."

She shook my hand like I just bought a car from her.

"Wait," I said, putting my weight on my good leg.

"I'm listening," she said, walking for her car.

"Were you related to Milly Molly?"

"Daughter."

She hiked up her jeans and walked around the front of her Ford GT. She descended perfectly the two tracks and blew a *bump-ba-ba-bump*. Her stereo blared Merle Haggard and I'm not so sure but a Coke can got stirred up as she went around the bad turn. She could not have thrown that out her window? Sure, she did. I picked her can up in the morning then checked on the treasure trove. All was gone, except for the gold earring that the root wore like wedding band.

I stood at the Cabot Trail in my blazer and glasses and I thought, "I am now one of the old fellows I saw as a boy, waiting for their ride, washed white and in ill-fitting clothes, ready to rove." My father would pull over when he came along these guys. "Jesus, look at the kids! No, thanks, Kenny, bai. Kerry Kilpatrick's on he's way and we're off ta Sydney! You take her easy now!"

Her Ford GT rumbled onto my Class A gravel; it was the very car I owned. She looked in her mirror before pulling out, climbed halfway out her window to see: "Jesus, Joseph, and Murray Joe! Why weren't ya kilt on this goddamn turn yet! Whatcha build here for, ta have people die when they were leavin' ya!" Her wheels climbed my sod, she squealed on asphalt.

I reached for the seat belt; it was a dangling strip.

"What are ya doin'? You don't need that," she said. "Thing got spread all over the place so I took the breadknife to her. I haven't had an accident in one year."

We flattened out on the road and motored.

"Ah," she said. "See? Person's gotta get out of here, least once a week, for sanity purposes. If they don't, look out!"

We drove in silence and I thought how of all them, this was the biggest mistake.

"And you, Miles? Miles and miles from home. Working on that cursed old hill, daylight till dark, day in, day out. Been in all those foreign places. Oh, I know. Everyone tries to get along without fanfare here. It's the culture, here. I got my property over across the Salt Lake so I'm not looking for anything. Paid for the thing, menial jobs, yalp — which I call *meaningful* jobs. I'm cheap and I squeak, so what? Built it meself. Woman — yes, me. No sir, no wriggling property out from under some old senior's nose. I've seen thum do that, lots. Nope, it's been my ambition to get along, slow and alone. But, you might as well hear it from me."

"Hear what?"

"I was a bit of a whore there for a while. Not too long." She elbowed me I don't know what for, but it struck the funny bone and stung all the way down Smokey and up through the North Shore. But long before I had to say, "You were?"

"We don't need to get in that, Miles. I wasn't paying attention and slipped past the age when a girl can get a fella with any sense. I just drank a while there and went home with whoever. Don't know how many times this old heart's been broke. Betcha there's thirty-five country albums in here. Nope. Cobbled all together somehow. Yes, and on my thity-fifth birthday I said, 'That's it, Argie! Get by on your frigging well own, sober!' I poured what I had down the sink and moved outta Mom's."

"That right?"

"I made a deal to take care of an old fella who was dying in return for a little piece of property. But we had that drawn up. Nope, I never went away either, nope. I did finish high school. Did rate well in high school. I knew your brothers, the younger ones. All you guys left. Came, were everywhere, then left like fleein' Egypt after the plague. Especially you. You, the only one to come back!"

The Englishtown Ferry churned toward us, its cable high out of the water. Evening light spread like warm honey as we sat in the little car I should have known, but didn't. Merle Haggard was on low and I was learning all about wardens and prisoners.

I said, "Did you throw a pop can out the window yesterday?"

"Who?" She made a production then of getting her ferry tickets from the upholstery strip near her sun visor. "Damn old tickets. Why do we even have a ferry here! 'Cause, I'll never know! Another government grab. These tickets cost twenty-five bucks! Last time I was on I saw the ticket man come to the fellow ahead of me. The fellow said, 'I don't need one — clergy.' Yeah, what about a graveyard worker? I near lost it."

We boarded the vessel as the sun was looking over a fence of black cloud. The ticket man with the wandering eye came to us, the same fellow from the puffin adventure. He winked a big eye and turned up his chin like he was sending a fly on its way. As boys, my brother said this man was peering into an ice-fishing hole when two smelt veered and it screwed up his eyes. My brother and I were young; we didn't understand loneliness and how all bodies that make it along long enough, go to pieces. I waved at the man and he touched his nose in some code of brotherhood. Puffin, woman, puffin? I don't know but there was brotherhood there.

Argyle Meaney and I stood at the movie posters.

"So that was you at your mother's funeral?" I said.

"That was me."

"And, at my father's?"

"I don't get along with the family. I didn't get along with her so much. I'm the youngest and the only one to stay. They're at each other's throats now over the property." She touched her cap. "So which movie's any good?"

"You're asking me?"

"Oh yeah. Gap, I suppose."

With my cold hand I pointed to one, the blazer giving zero heat.

"Go home!" she said.

"There, then. That one, then."

"Go home!"

I was distracted by the passing cars, by horns, and people, but mostly by the fact that Argyle had just put her hand on my arm. It was the first contact in as long as I could remember; she couldn't have known how it set me off like cat aboard a rocking boat.

We got inside and the lights went down. The soundtrack started and in flickering light I saw how Argyle Meaney was all set to enjoy this. She had her bucket of popcorn and half-liter of pop, no ice. She had been with all those fellows but there was none of this, she said, not a night like this. This was an outing. She seemed a good companion to me, laughing, carrying on, team-spirited. She ate her popcorn one at a time, took in all the soundtrack offered, and peered at every frame. It seemed the last picture show on earth for her so she was making a go of it.

I settled in to watch, crossed my arms, leaned left. I tried to see what was going on up there in Hollywood. There's a car chase. Someone's dead. That girl's waking up with combed hair. But then, all that majesty of landscape without going to it, the good clothes and easy words.

Over a cheeseburger she said, "Excuse me." I guess it was a burp because a big-knuckled hand covered her mouth. "Guess I'm nervous," she said, her eyes were closer together than I had thought; I could see so well in the fast-food joint's light. She dipped a fry in my ketchup blob.

"You over there with your picks and shovels and wheel-barrows. And I don't know what, going. If we don't hear your chainsaw then it's your fiddle. Look, I keep my mouth shut. People know about the time you had. It scares them and they stay away. Might even anger some. I work in the graveyard and have a job as long as I want."

Other couples ate cheeseburgers and talked at tables. I was a part of that.

"A job is gold," I said.

"Exactly the way I see it."

"Quite the name, though, Argyle."

"Our family was that big it's all that was left. They were gonna call me Jason. But you just try to get one of those these days, a job. Breaking the law, maybe. And it's good work, grave-yarding, outdoors, movin' your body. Takes the bitchiness rate out of a person and how many of us have that in short supply? I got my investments. House is paid off, for one, oh, I don't know how many years back now."

"That is an accomplishment."

"I got all my floor-to-ceiling windows when they were replacing the old ones in the Keltic. I nabbed one of the old Highland Bungalow cabins when they offered them for the taking. I hired a truck from Sydney to come down for that. I put a storey on, got a foundation underneath. Bank wouldn't give me a mortgage till a foundation was under her. The bank likes their concrete. It's the finish work that costs ya."

"How about kids?"

"What do you mean? Oh, who? Me? Jesus, no."

I could only keep my eyes approximately on her because she was staring straight at me like she was giving it to the judge — that is, except for this last bit, about the kids. I didn't mean anything by it. But her eyes were back on me and I had to perform again.

"Because," she said. "I see how the man, how the woman is! She's the cat who don't care to be held or looked upon till she herself wants it. Yalp, lineup stretching from Glace Bay to Halifax with cats. You guys? Well now, you're on the mutt team, carrying around all that guilt from room to room. Tell me the last time you saw a cat with guilt? No one told you this before but I happen to also know a fella likes the odd hot meal, the odd fishcake, his towel folded. And you want someone to pick up after themselves. Answer the phone. I know, I know! Someone to hover when that friend you have over is not gettin' the hint. There's utility in someone like me. Ho, mister! Don't you well worry about it, I know the game."

"Sounds like it."

"When you're versed in it, when you think it through. Which is what makes me different. The deal's to keep your mouth shut and enjoy the ride. But that applies to both."

"Mouth shut, eh?"

"What? Talkin' a lot?"

"No, no, no."

She may have flirted with her hair right here. I'm not one to know. She did take three fries, dip them in my ketchup again and put them in her mouth. She touched the corners of her mouth with a serviette then, like she was raised at the table of the royal family. And I never saw anyone do it, but then she used vinegar over a napkin on the table to clean her fingertips.

"Those the glasses?" she said.

"These? Why, do you know about these?"

"No, not at all. And not about Charlie, either."

"This is them."

I wanted to think with longing of my house, of my fiddle and little guitar, the good old-fashioned fire I'd get goin' soon as I got in the door. No longing came.

"Then hold still," she said. She was coming forward. I thought there was an eyelash on my nose. "My hands are clean," she said. I looked off to the side through my lenses. And with her fingers near my ears, she brought my face to mid-table. She leaned till I could smell ketchup; a fry was in my hand. "Hold," she said and she kissed me, on the mouth. "That's what a person calls a kiss. I couldn't take it, Miles. You're friggin' gorgeous! What? How?"

I eased back, she was still forward. "Let them look all they want. I don't care if they look. How did they come into the world?" She addressed the audience. "That was our first kiss in Sydney!"

A worker clapped.

"Ah my," she said looking around, her cap upside down on her lap. "See, I went for it. Won't be the same now. And all that Hollywood one-night-stand-business? Not in these parts."

I don't know if it was the absence of the seat belt or my ill-fitting sports coat that made me feel so exposed. There was another feeling, a mixed feeling of comfort and reassurance. My toes tingled and I moved them in my dress shoes on that ferryboat ride. Argyle dug for my hand as we went down that lonesome old North Shore stretch, with its mist-filled street-lights of bingo-marker gold. She held my hand, held it in the fashion of fingers being knit. Her touch was manual in grip but I knew tenderness and even care. And those were there. I thought of the burp, that excusing of herself, her dancing grey eyes rate close together staring at me. How can I get this hand back? What will that moment be like? Yes, all was rough peace in the light of the dash, in the tiny spring snowsquall before the hairpin turns of Smokey. She laid my hand aside before ramming her gearshift forward, her transmission heated, doing a wonderful job.

At the foot of the driveway she said out her window, "I won't climb up in there with ya just yet, Miles. But you remember this good time we had, hear me?"

"I will, Argyle. Easy on that gravel and I don't want to ever have to pick up a pop can down here again."

She gunned it to get across the bad turn, hit her *beep-ba-beep-beep* along with a *bump-ba-ba-bump*. I left the Cabot Trail, climbing slow with my limp, getting to the apple tree and stopping to put up an arm. "Tim, oh, Tim, oh, Tim. Just when a person thinks all the foolishness is dead and buried."

My hand was getting better. I had received the last of the shots in Neils Harbour. The antibiotics were long gone and I had listened to Sammy say how it was important to take all the antibiotics not just a few — or none, as the old guys did. I could just fashion a G and a C, and if I was lucky, a D. I lifted Old Eleven, strummed a G, a C and somehow managed to peddle to the night "The Twister".

> *I remember when we met*
> *How you did confess*
> *That you were a gamble*
> *I would never lose*
> *You waltzed yourself right in*
> *Helped yourself to my gin*
> *And now I can't find*
> *That bottle anywhere.*

The Geese Are Leaving Today

Chirpy the Chipmunk owned my house for a while in the early building stage. In the city I had been staying in the closet of a Mexican student named Omar. It was winter; I was poor, he was poor. But I trusted him with my songs and we sang. He added all kinds of Mexican harmonies to fill his bachelor space. He offered me beans and bacon while talking about loving "smashed potatoes" and to watch out for the cops or they will "kiss your ass!"

When I came back that spring I had to get through an eight-foot snowdrift that blocked my boarded-up door and inside, covered half the living room. Chirpy spotted me in the new light and flew off the handle. No way was he leaving! And what the hell was I doing, invading his space! Why did I stand in his home, full-sized and ignorant of the state of affairs!

He rattled pans, kicked over a coffee canister, scurried across the wall like a Satan child, calling out every expletive in the squirrel dictionary. I threw a pot. "Get out of here, you! This is my house, squirrel! I didn't spend seventy thousand dollars on timber and windows to house your little brown ass!" He chattered, denounced me, and I had to make a charge for him. Well, you know the rest. Except I had no DNA lab on it. Maybe Chirpy is still out there squatting in someone else's home, getting drunk on their rotten peanuts.

Argyle Meaney called in six weeks.

"Well," she said.

"Well what, Argyle — the water pump's all apart. Well, what?"

"You got one past the goalie is what."

"What goalie? I hate hockey, what're ya talking about?"

"You'll know in a few months, Pop soda."

She hung up and I put down the phone. Pop soda? Oh — Pop soda. Ut, oh. Why did I feel so young, so young and so arrested? My mother and father both in the grave, yet that feeling I knew when they lived, of having done something criminal again — that's what filled my chest. Argyle, forty-two years old, and pregnant for the first time. My mind went to the hour before Tim Dickey climbed down to his seaside hammock of the eternal. "Jesus, bai! You're getting her!" he said. "You play that old fiddle real good now! Good, for my ears at least. The old man'd like her. Oh, I feel like a drink."

I looked at him.

"Another, I mean. I always do when I hear that music."

Tim was at the fridge, his finger on the opening of a letter held by a Korean-mask magnet: "Dear Tenant 6 — You, eh, Miles? — Dear Tenant 6, I am writing you regarding a concern both my roommate and myself have expressed regarding the noise level coming from your apartment. Since I have lived here, in September 2001, I have always been able to hear your violin playing, especially stomping along to keep the beat . . . " He waved the paper. "Ha! You were playing at 6:00 AM! Nice hour! So that's the larger world, eh Miles?" He read on. "Wow! Stomp! She likes that word!" He put the paper back on the fridge.

"That why you here, Miles? To stomp?"

"I believe it is, Tim. And the next day I did drop by her apartment — as she invites me there, for a discussion. Except I was in my underwear and half-bearded. I got locked out of my apartment doing the laundry below and had to ask to use her phone."

"Holy dying, Jesus! Go on! Me son! That must have been nice sight! Was she mortified? Oh, man. He forsakes the city lights, pretty girls, and shop windows for snow, woods, and an hour into Sydney to buy a tomato, a carrot, and a dozen eggs. All so he can stomp. Well, Jesus. And here I was thinking anyone coming here was on the run from something. I expect you'll find everything here you do anywheres else, though. Trouble-wise."

I played and Tim danced. He was good. He sure was on that hyper side of his bi-polarity, I believe they call it, because in the next instant it was like he had just watched the *Titanic* go down. He didn't finish his dance but dropped his arms and, sad as hell, sat by the fire.

"I know about that time you had, Miles. I just like to go on with foolishness. I'll never know how you made it. None here will. But I don't know how anyone makes anything. I got this season affective disorder, SAD they call it. Sad, all right. I like to call it GLAD when I 'Get dee liquor added'!" Tim's eyes went crystal like a doll's. Then he got sad. "And to have kids — Miles? That breaks your heart worse than anything. All the hope and promise needed. And you got nothing to give it."

I was on the couch, staring at the ceiling timbers. I had painted it white up there but it needed another coat. It would be better to close the place in; that coyote lady was right. Ceilings need to close. That cathedral ceiling business is for the birds. So much in a house needs closing. The primary factor in a house is coziness; shutting brings it together. To hell with the looks. And also, I have been frozen over here for how many years now I don't even know anymore. Yes, closing it heats it, too.

I turned for my father's journal: *The hardest thing I ever done was obey my father. He told me the dog was hit by a car and he was too weak himself to take it to the island. We lived on the Freshwater Lake before the Park set their Expropriation in motion. I carried the dog to the water and my father carried the rifle and the shovel. I rowed the dog out and I know they all heard the shot.*

I called Argyle.

"Did I say that I heard you, Miles? Because I did! Nothing changes. We'll get a crib for here and for there, if you want it. You come visit when you want. Your hill's your country. Across the harbour here at the sinkholes and copper needles is mine. Yours too, if you want it. Jesus, man, we ain't no spring chickens. What's there left to guard against? I said how it would be when I met you and what's a person got but their word? We'll handle it the way it should be handled always, straightforward and head on. What religious group, society, or law of the land do we need to satisfy, us? We're those junco birds you're fond of — just gettin' on with it. Tell you the truth, I think you're happy, Miles. That's what I think."

"I was never sad, Argyle."

"You know what I mean. Because that's what I saw when I laid eyes on you, care. And don't worry about the trouble this'll cause for me at the graveyard."

"What trouble?"

"What trouble? Pregnant and unwed? Oh, no trouble, a-tall! Big unwed belly mowing over the Catholic graves? You just watch the good old fuss, though, I'll kick up if they do give a person grief. I can write a letter, an email, knock on a door. I wouldn't wanna have to deal with me."

"Yes." I stared ahead, a man just aboard the train for the Gulag.

"All right, Argyle," I said. "You are right, though."

"And as for those dried-up apple-heads, our professional gossips . . . What's never sat straight with me is how when the story is real good, juicy good, how powerless they get. This is juicy good. Around-the-world Miles, a father. But really though. A little baby? 'Cause that's all it is, a kitten you got to get a saucer to. Love's what that is. A little love project. Miles, I go to bed every night with tears on my face, every night. I'm so happy. I'm so happy you entered my life."

"*I* entered *your* life?"

"You taught that Franklin and Frankolene to fly over and steal my lunch, fly off with my bracelet."

"Yeah, right. What the doctor say? About your health?"

"Who? Me? Someone who works outside? A horse, Miles, a horse. He said I'm good. But I gotta go, my show's on. Door's wide open . . . Put too much of a fire on, partly the reason. No, you play that fiddle or trumpet or whatever else it is you got over there tonight so I can hear it. It sounds really, really good from a distance, like a line thrown to a mariner lost at sea. Drop in after."

I looked across the harbour at the fog surrounding her one light. She never turned it off, only replaced the bulb. She lived in a house that was finished, so the kid won't freeze at least. I drew my bow and played for all that fog and all that mist and all the thickness in the gold and the silver of the lights over there, in the kitchens and living rooms, rising from the banks of the Woody Shore. But then the worst kind of rain struck and the old sticky wood and strings got wet where I stood at the open door trying to finish, "The Cape Smokey March". Full night was on.

I went to the fridge and got the huge hunk of cake and frosting. I opened the kitchen window with my free hand, feeling the pull down my leg; I was stiff tonight from the bites. I didn't fight it but how quick you become fragile and slow to heal. I threw the cake out onto the wet grass, its inch of frosting breaking on impact. Sammy's wife, Clara, had dropped off the cake, but ever since learning about Argyle's diabetes and what she went through I was off the sugar.

I looked at the cake and thought how twenty crows will be on that by morning. One sat in a birch now past the box of light thrown from the kitchen. It sat in a dark driving rain awaiting its chance. It wasn't old Broken Wing, Old Franklin. Franklin had his left wing always tucked in hard and his head always squeezed low for the warmth of his breast. This crow was young. It wasn't Frankolene for sure. I watched him shut the camera obscura of his eye, open it to stare at me. But his wing did look a little damaged. Maybe I was wrong.

I got my glasses and spoke out the window crack, "Cranky Frank? Hello. Hello." The crow stayed where he was. I trained the flashlight on him. No, not Frank, too young, too starved. The cake was not manageable. I threw the poor bastard a piece of donut that he swooped for, then flew down over the built-up field in the dark rain to disappear from sight. But my eyes picked up the decoy — Howl the Owl on that second ant-eaten spruce at the foot of the driveway. He was in silhouette, but watched. All watched tonight, it seemed. Tonight and every night.

Of the birds around me, the one I had to attach myself to was Argyle. The woman was a pure nut bar. She was from a big family and the only one to stay. I was from a big family and the only one to return.

I carried an armload of books up to bed, plus the current red I had going from the Five Feet.

I didn't need to call her to say I wouldn't be over. There was rain on the driveway. I was getting closer and closer all the time in the climb up to the house with my tracks.

I opened the upstairs window and breathed in the pine I had planted, soaked and scented in the rain it came; sea mist entered soft as satin and the weather bell for the Gut, Lonesome Louise, cried her pretty eyes out tonight. I turned for the green and the right-red-return marine buoys out there protecting all hulls backing off from a black ocean.

Argyle, Argie. *Figura*, is what Brazilians call a character. The rasp in her voice perked me up. Action and joy were her partners. But all the hard times, the loneliness she must have faced in the life she had lived. The abandonment, the passage of time. The half-faced guys during her party times must never have seen the goodness, or saw it, but contemplated none of it. Their dismissal had saved her for me. Argyle, the mother? She will be the best there is. Because when she wasn't talking, she could actually listen. She could tell you of an incident that you had spoken of but forgotten you had. When she mentioned it, though, the incident was humorous or meaningful. And hearing it come back to you let you see that it was someone's life — yours. And it seemed good. It showed that the other she was with meant a lot to her. The feeling was that the big moment had come to her life because she had found someone to trust. Her arms going akimbo, that laugh loud enough to be heard across the water. She was not waiting for later; her life was the moment in front of her. I made her laugh. I loved that. And she was ready for change, if someone "with sense was in the picture," as she said. It would be a sight to see her dance — because she had spoken of wanting to. She hated dancing, she said, but it was supposed to be good for you and for your place in society. She read this. I wouldn't mind seeing Argyle sway to music. I laughed myself to sleep over it — her whirling, scrunching up her face as she did her best move, a hip lift and arm extension. Oh, I laugh now till tears are on my pillow and sleep has come. No, don't get excited. No sleep tonight.

I went to the second floor and got by the fire. I grabbed the Little Old Eleven and looked at the sketches I had put on it. I moved my fingers for "The Geese Are Leaving Today".

The geese are leaving today
The sky their own highway
Now they're leaving too
Just like you
But they'll be back one day.

The Man in the Moon

One day on a steep slope of rock maple I saw a bear in a tree. All by himself a game of mewling he played, of pawing an ear and babbling to a leaf. The tree was probably a ten-year-old maple, jammed in the ground of a forest scant, in a hollow with light dappled. No bird sang and a greater silence grew beyond. The bear stretched for a branch to see just how far this paw of his could go. He moved his head with the foliage, a hippie bear with not a care in the world. But something was near him: a pair of eyes watched. He looked at me a full second before turning back to his narcotic branch. I shifted and this he heard. He sniffed the air — a black bear can smell food up to a kilometre away. This one had not been paying attention. So like the lithest of monkeys he swung from his tree and bounced up over the ridge, agile, determined. I found no footprint but turned from my investigation after realizing I was in the woods with a bear and far, far from home.

It was late October and sopping leaves held the road. The harbour was a blister blue and rain bits sang into it. I had just buried Franklin after finding him in the built-up field. I set him up by the cabin in a place with a view. I drove around the harbour and turned in for the sinkholes. Argyle made us a sandwich of tuna and alfalfa sprouts on homemade bread. I watched her operate the can opener.

"Listen," she said. "That dance — "

"Ho, ho."

"No, wait. It's on the other side of the island. No one'll ever even know we were there." She was looking at me. "What, I'm no different from you? Dancing? Dancing's the dose! It's just we need to see people. But it's more than that — people go nuts when they don't dance. Every society in the world has it in some form. Mental health, that's what's involved. And a dance brings people together."

"To fight."

"Not over there. We're talking fiddle music."

"Then we're also talking square dancing."

"They'll show us. My belly doesn't show. We won't even dance if that's the case, just watch."

"It's another country over there, Argyle."

"Mabou?"

"Jesus! Is it there? You don't want a person intimidated or nothing." She knew she had me. "Listen, one word about me playing the fiddle and watch how out I walk. Those people are way too serious about their music. Argyle Meaney? Agreed?" She was wrong; she was beginning to show. It was going to be a big baby if you asked me. Argyle would fit in; she always fit in. Someone like that was valuable. I ate the sandwich. Was it ever good.

We boarded the Englishtown Ferry. I drove.

"We are doing it, Miles. Just how I said. You in your place, me in mine."

For anyone listening, this exchange would have sounded strange. I do know, though, what she was talking about. We had got her wood in, then mine. She had me eating better food and even putting on weight. I fixed a running toilet and hung her porch door.

"And we don't need any more than what we got, okay? Promise me."

"You're the girl all the guys want."

"I told you I was."

I felt I should not keep her at the distance I did, as I'd had everything else. I handed the collector the booklet and he actually said, "How long yous two been goin' out?" Argyle gave a smile to the glass.

"Spring," I said, tapping my wheel, taking back the booklet; I whistled a b-flat and got the window up. He was younger than the old guy but there was something similar in the hang of his clothes.

"That guy?" said Argyle. "He comes to my window every time and talks the whole trip across. Poor guy. You in here."

"A thousand sad and one happy, eh, Argyle?"

"What do you mean by 'a thousand'?"

The ferry carried us across Saint Anne's Bay and we listened to *Cape Breton Connection*, a show of local tunes and big local accents that had us tune into Ireland, the Shetlands, and Wales all at the same time. There was mention of the dance. The car climbed the ramp and we drove past the ornamental grass where I had laid the puffin.

We were lost on a back road on the west side of the island. Argyle rolled down her window. "I know it's cold, Miles! But it's what they said at the garage! Roll your window down and listen."

"How can I listen when you're smacking on that big lumberjack sandwich you bought from them? You think that stuff is good for a baby?"

"Go on — little treat."

Our car lights lit the sides of a mossy church where long-legged teenagers in big boots had plastic cups. We locked our doors and crunched gravel for the hill; hoots and hollers floated for us.

"Here's where we're kilt," said Argyle and I stayed quiet. I knew she had never been on an outing like this and that she had put it together for my benefit. She drew up the zipper of her coat, wrapped herself better in the black jacket I bought her on credit. But she had on her Husqvarna chainsaw cap, screwed it left then right, her bouffant hair Afro-ing a hallelujah at the sides. She had washed her hair for this but was past the age when hair settles after a rinse. As if about to address the Knights of Columbus she cleared her throat, then said nothing. We entered the hall. The two of us were as suited to this place as a couple of hot buns in a toolbox.

Fluorescent lights lit the foyer where there was a stocking hat and a hand-drawn sign: *Just Ten Bucks!* We passed through an interior door to see a circle of men and women wait on a hardwood floor. The place was lit like a runway. Square dance, all right, and no hiding in dim light like on our side of the island.

The dance circle held hands, swept for centre, and backed off like jellyfish near the wharf. A violinist and a piano player worked from a little stage. The violinist was in either pajamas or a suit. He leaned back to communicate to his piano player, who wore a dress and corsage. Eyeing us on the periphery were seated folk and, with clairvoyant certainty, I heard the same two words go like tumbling cards: "Who's that?" We stood under raw light, two labourers in from the hay.

A pair of dancers left the circle.

"Take off your jacket," said Argyle. "Put mine there."

"Why?"

She had my forearm, was drawing me out.

"Hup," I said. "Argyle!"

The lights stayed bright. She and I were inserted in with the dancers. It was the moment I knew I would break up with her, here in the company of Mabou-ers and Inverness-ers heated from dance.

"Grab her hand there!" said Argyle. And to me closely, she said, "What're are ya worried about? Half them got a foot in the grave and the other on a banana peel."

"Which is where I'll be, after I die of embarrassment. Argyle, come on. Let's get a couple of drinks. We had an agreement."

"We will. Here, take my hand. I'm not drivin' two hours to sit on them bingo chairs."

I hated it, every sway, every clip, every clop. The ride home I would break up with her. My mother loved the word mortified. That pretty well describes it, clasping these Cape Breton Scottish palms in this snaky circle. We bumped elbows, shoulders struck, kneecaps; we missed hands. And then, oh my Jesus, that foolish part where everyone drops their arms and step dances it out all on their own. I called up old black and white movies where an old fellow in short-legged overalls hung thumbs through shoulder straps and kicked a big set of bare feet. I tried to stay casual about it. Argyle was all over the place. "Please," I told myself, "Don't be as bad as her!" But we were back in the walking of it again, the exchanging of hands, ending again with different partners. The fiddler was looking, piano player gawking. I didn't even have the courage to see how it registered on the faces of the seated folk.

DAVID DOUCETTE

Square dance, all right, Argyle and me had it square, rectan-
gular, and rhomboid. Then came that part where you go down,
with your partner, past two lines. Argyle ran it, to catch me. I
couldn't help it, I laughed till tears came because she smacked
face and eyes into a woman and near flattened her. An old man
huffed like a blowfish and walked off.

I started to walk off, too, when Argyle hollered to cease all
music: "Where you going?"

"Off the floor is where!"

"But you didn't even learn it yet!"

"And you did?"

The hall erupted in laughter. Square dancers wiped their
eyes and looked at each other in faces, it seemed, for the first
time. The fiddler was on his feet, "She's right! Get back out
here, you! That was just Willy McMaster leaving! He's off to
the bathroom!"

Encouragement came from all corners and I knew the truth
of the seated folk: that Argyle and I represented them — they
wanted to be up dancing too but skill or maybe good sense kept
them back. We clearly had neither.

Someone had a hand on my shoulder, a priest in a collar and
V-neck. "Finish the set at least. She wants you to." This priest
replaced Willy McMaster and the music resumed. For another
few whirls we went around till I said the hell with it and got
to dancing and clapping and hooting like I don't know what
except that that's how it feels you're supposed to express it.

Jesus — me, Argyle, doing the big hand exchange, and
catching on. And when it came to that step dance part I
really tried to feel the music in my feet. I believe I was smiling.
Something had beaten me here, fair and square. I looked at
Argyle. She smiled with thin lips. That's what it is to have
someone.

But Argyle remained a sight. She had that one move I knew she had: the hip lift. I keeled over at the sight. She had grabbed her cap for it, on her feet were the ladies version of Kodiaks, her jeans cuffed, her laces snapping at people. She did a shuffle that had people pull back. Tears splashed my glasses. Joy, joy, joy and I didn't know why it came so intensely except it was connected to that baby, one I would tell all this to. Little hands were in there now probably grabbing a hold of the sides: "Jesus, nice ride! What the hell's goin' on out there!"

It was done, the circle resolved. But you know what? Another started and we stayed up. We had the basics and with the help of experienced dancers we soon looked the part. We didn't drink; we paraded and stepped and held hands the whole night through. But at last the fiddler rose. He wiped sweat with a hanky.

He called out, "Where yous two from?"

"You mean to dance so well?" said Argyle. "He plays."

"Argyle!" I said.

"Who?" said the fiddler.

"Him, the fiddle."

"Ar-jesus-gyle," I muttered.

Off the stage came the fiddler, holding out his instrument and bow. "Go up." The piano player passed. "Go on up," she said. "I'm done out. I'll listen from the canteen."

Argyle, with her Japanese Jesus manga eyes, was pretending to look at the seated folk. In a three-piece suit, necktie, and fedora, the oldest fellow in the hall pipes up, "They're tellin me ya play! Well, sir, that's the bargain here in Cape Breton — dance or don't dance but if ya play ya gotta play!" Maybe it was his wife who took his arm and whispered to him, prompting him to shout, "Ingonish! Well now, what are you talking about? Very

best of fiddlers from over there! Get up — 'cause I ain't leavin'
till I hear a little a the Ingonish flavour!"

A gent whose hand I had grabbed many times in the
exchange of partners said, "You won't get out alive. Better grab
the fiddle." Another hand capped my forearm — I was a toy
all the kids were having a go at. "Okay, okay," I said because I
couldn't take the contact.

Ah my, dancing was one thing; this here was a whole other
level of violation. I looked at Argyle, who winked like we were
partners on a game show. I remembered her brother Harrison
in the graveyard, "Construction — I know, Miles. I wasn't
much for work. That thing you run from, though, I learned is
what you got to turn and face." Damn it all, these truths and
chances, pulling at you. "Okay, okay."

Yes, I played. For people all over the world I played but, aside
from those two funerals, never on the island. I played for birds,
for foxes, crows, and eagles. I played for my village across the
water, the yacht below the birches, but I was hiding in those
cases; the village was a couple kilometres away. I did play for
Paul McCartney's yacht, docked down below the house that
summer he had the Halifax show. He had come north for peace
and quiet. I pulled out an old civil-war trumpet and wailed
away: *Yesterday, all my troubles* . . . Portholes snapped shut and
the ship left through the night. For the writers of the fridge-
magnet letter, I played. And for Tim I played.

"That's too bad — piano player's gone?" I told them, in a
final effort to get out of it.

"I know a C!"

It was Argyle. And the lines of the break-up speech were
written and rehearsed. I gave her a dirty look.

"I know a C," she said. "You got a whole career going if you got a C chord." She wasn't using my name. "Come on, you! I'm the one at risk. Eh, everyone?"

We sat on the stage, the violin on my shoulder. I was feeling hugely tired. Argyle clamped down on her C, hit it three times and on the fourth got another note mixed in. But she held her head high, shoulders back. Amadeus Mozart, about to dish it out.

"G!" I said. "G!" I was in the second turn of "Garret Doyle's Jig". Oh, hell, I just bore down to see what would happen. Argyle did find a rhythm, though, and in a scold I told her to hold that, right there, and not back off! I played over the top of it and gained some semblance. But there it was, we had something with "Coralee's March", followed by "After The Funeral" and "Keats' Reel". "The Smokey Tunes" brought it all together. I had brought her over to the key of *D*. You can rest when you're in that.

"How's the day going," people ask; "It's going," comes the answer. This was like that. But it was going for Inverness county ears, the best in the land for fiddle appreciation. Yet chins rose, nodding came to heads, I saw feet keep time. The thing I knew is that is all you ever have to do is make people feel.

We were not the caliber they knew yet these big hearts clapped. And what's that? Ah, for Jesus sake — they were forming a circle! And now, moving arms and legs to it! Oh no — Argyle was caught up in the sight and she kicked her chair back, got on her feet, pregnant, to play diminished, sevenths, ninths, augmented — demented! The more mistakes the better! She pounded keys, flew down black, up white!

"Hut!" she hollered. "Hut! Hoo! Hoohaw!" Down the *D*, up the *G*, down the *A*. And when she forced me back into that dreaded C scale, the one empty of feel, I felt we lost it. But the circle danced and stayed up.

My eye caught the fiddler at the entrance. He hooted, kicked up a heel, was having a grand time, cup in his teeth, hands clapping. Argyle's Husqvarna chainsaw cap dropped onto her keyboard so she really messed me up and the two of us turned those centuries of Cape Breton fiddle music into someone damaging a symphony hall with a five-pound maul. But folks danced and we got her done. Best ten dollars ever spent!

"Dere, me son! What a yas tink a dat?" said Argyle, fumbling with her cap to get it on, to tame that big head of hair. "Tole yas he could play! He's closing on fifty and is just now's goin' to be a father!"

"What?" said a woman. "Yous two got a baby comin'?"

"First," said Argyle. "For both of us."

A round of applause went; they laughed, nodded, clapped, complimented. I had to answer questions like we had just won the Oscar. And I don't believe I've had so much physical human contact. Ever.

In the car there wasn't a person in the hall we didn't talk about. Argyle wished she hadn't mentioned the baby.

"Why not?" I said. "They liked that part the best."

"I'm old. You get to blabbing too much when you're feeling good. Miles? Is there something we should talk about?"

I looked over. She looked over. I dropped my eyes for the sad bare fingers of her hand.

"Oh, no," she said. "Although I wouldn't mind. What you went through, Miles."

"I don't talk about that."

"But it's important to."

"It's not important to. Where did you learn that from, your show? Then it must be the way, then."

"I did learn it from my show. Not everyone can read five feet of books. But they have to get their knowledge from some place."

"I'm reading those because your mother got a promise out of me!"

"All right, all right. You won't ever hear me talk of it again. Just know you got someone to listen." She laughed and said she was glad to live to see the day I played the fiddle over in Inverness County. I told her she was right, that I would never have done it without her. But weight held back our conversation. She had me pull over, got out, and threw up in the ditch.

"Lumberjack sandwiches," she said returning. "Never again."

"Well, what are ya eatin' them for?"

"What am I eatin' them for? They're good. They were good."

At the ferry, I got out and puffed on half of a Colts cigar Looie had left. I asked the ticket collector about the old fellow. "Heart attack," he said refusing to look toward the Rocket. He turned to me instead, "He was my old man."

Back in the car, Argyle's hair was all over the place. She smoothed what she could but it made not the slightest difference in the world. "We'll stick her up at your place," she said. "I ain't got the room," she said.

"Stick who up at my place?"

"The piano. The whole seventy, eighty, ninety keys of her. Time to start living, Miles. You can get them for the hauling in Sydney."

"I don't know what you would call what we're doing if it's not living."

"But a piano is real livin'."

But I knew what she meant. The wave-on to exit came from the ticket collector, though we were the only ones on the ferry. We scraped the car bottom on the ramp, easing from the rocking vessel with its exposed cable. We left the black wavelets to pass up a salty slip and the Rocket zoomed past the cable house for stars that shone like poked holes in a kettledrum.

By the woodstove Argyle drank mint tea for the baby. I started a song that had her interrupting, "I hope that isn't you in this song!" I sang on "The Man in the Moon".

> *I told you darling*
> *That I would be home late*
> *But you didn't listen*
> *You wouldn't wait*
> *No supper on the table*
> *No wine in the glass*
> *Our furnished apartment*
> *A museum at last.*

Goodbye Old Loneliness

One time I was on my hands and knees in a thicket. I was on the top of the mountain in a place so dense with spruce that it drove me further and further toward the ground. Needles scratched my face and my stocking hat got lifted off. I squeezed through a tiny opening to get out. When I did, when I brushed off my knees and stood, a massive moose's vapour from flared nostrils hit my forehead and face. I did not look into the eyes. I bowed, knelt, and reversed into the thicket.

It was Christmas, a year since the attack, and I called Argyle, "Road's still open to the beach, I'll pick you up." Down on the hard sand we looked at the cold fog around the bill of Smokey. Middlehead stretched for the icy water of the bay and a cold sky set all off, blue and clean in every direction.

"Argyle. See that seagull? That's what you look like."

"You shut up, you."

We held mittened hands and walked in our heavy boots. We had the same pair, felted, white ones that came to our knees. We got a deal in town but you had to buy two pairs.

"I can't go through another year," I said.

She looked at me. "Well, I hope you can."

"I don't want a little bastard."

She stopped, her cheeks were red in the cold.

"I got no money," I said. "But I was thinking of going nearby for Christmas and maybe gettin' married."

She put her mittens to her face and spoke in them. I pulled them down and saw she was an old girl but so happy in her wrinkles that she had me smile.

"You'd do that for me?" she said.

"I'd do it for me. Of course I would."

"We don't need a dime," she said.

"That's good 'cause I don't have one."

"We take my car, though, when it's out of Doucette's. Your transmission's shot."

"Deal there."

We drove up over Smokey in a snowstorm but the North Shore got reasonable. We boarded the ferry and we quieted when we saw the ticket collector. A woman came over to get our ticket.

We found a priest in the North Sydney Yellow Pages and got married after a couple double-doubles at Tim Horton's. The afternoon cost fifty bucks. We spent Christmas in Louisburg at a drafty bed-and-breakfast on the sea, then hit the stores for Boxing Day. I got Argyle a ring. She chipped in, but got the one she wanted. They said it was a Canadian diamond, one from under the Canadian Arctic. "Yalp," I said. "Right!" But if there was any truth to it, I liked the idea. It felt good to fill up that third left finger of hers. I watched her touch the ring the whole trip home. "First and last I'll ever wear," she said. It was then I knew marriage was a big deal, that people put real emotion in it. Argyle was awful big by this point.

"Need anything around the harbour?" The voice came up to where I worked around a frozen cabin bank.

"Not a thing, Sammy. Thanks, bud." I had sounded accommodating and it worked. I heard his truck haul its heavy ass away. It was winter, the trees were knocking, the crows catching high cold drafts to sail over backward.

The stone wall for the shower was complete. I was framing it with heavy timber, covering it with a wood roof. More and more I wanted to stay in this cabin. I was freer over here. I was above the sea, in woods meeting a mountain, hidden. Frozen earth was only inches below the floorboards. I would look over to the main house and see the weight of a bank, Scotiabank.

"You up there?"

"I'm good, Sammy, thanks. I don't need a thing."

"Yeah, but I'm back because they told me to tell you to get to the hospital. That she's having it."

"No, not yet."

"Oh, yes. She's there."

"I'm coming."

"Miles? You're up there like a mad person. Stop now, stop the digging."

"I'm not digging, Sammy. I said, I'm coming."

"You driving that old car down?"

At the road I reassured Sammy, shovelling out the Rocket, getting in and pulling for north.

At the ski hill, I entered sun. She said she'd phone. We talked the night before and I was supposed to drive her there. I bet she drove herself down last night. Ha, tricked by my own tricks — let none in, do it all yourself. "Don't worry," she'd said. "I'm going to make this easy on you." I had told her to stop saying that.

I geared down. I was through the village and climbing Little Smokey. Snow had started and was falling hard but I was in the Park again, with its good plowed roads and plenty of salt. More snow struck nearing the top of Little Smokey. I flicked on

the wipers, cranked up the heater. The transmission was suffi-
ciently warm, though labouring. It was a car you couldn't kill.

But the Twin Hills had her creep again and after clearing
those I zoomed past Black Brook to meet whiteouts. I was taking
that trip my parents took me on, years and years back with a
fever, to this thing called a hospital. "You're sick. We can't do
anything for you and need to go north. Say your prayers with
us on Little Smokey and be brave because there will be hospital
smells to scare you."

Nothing rattled Argyle. She could do it all. Little things
rattled her. She tripped over a branch she had not lopped off
properly and with tears said, "I fell, Miles." It was such a sad
look, one that said, "Help me up, because I'm realizing I can't
do it all." Is that it? That you finally meet your other self? And
watching that person, that you are, tells you where you have
gone wrong. Is it the only way you will see yourself?

I drove into the hospital parking lot and saw up close the
place in which I'd been born. It was the place where I was
stitched up after the fall off the monkey bars; sewn up after my
brother Joe opened my head with a garden hoe as we searched
for worms to sell; on Halloween Paddy struck me with the big
rock, too. Of course, there were the coyotes.

A stooped big-breasted woman in the hospital entrance put
her black eye on me. "Come in the fresh air, Miles." She zipped
up a thin winter coat and walked past me.

It was ten below outside, a cutting sleet coming off the
Atlantic. I saw the woman was old and, though probably not
a nurse, was nurse-ly. She lit a smoke as winter breakers struck
the cold sand of Neils Harbour beach. But she beckoned me in
a little further, to a nook out of the wind at a smoker's can. She
smelled of sterilizing alcohol, and the game of syringes and of
stitches came back.

"You don't remember me. I'm Greta Daisley. You got a boy, Miles."

"I do?"

"Miles?"

"Go ahead."

"We lost her."

"Argyle?"

"From the start she was so fragile and there was hemorrhaging. The baby was oversized because it had been getting too much sugar. They called me when she came in early. They say she slipped away before anyone had a chance to turn around. I knew your mother. What a woman to have raised that big group. I was there to bring you into the world. Your mother would have been proud of you, of all of you. I told them I'd be the one to tell you. She came to me, see. All she talked about was a natural birth and about you. Miles. I'm so sorry, dear."

I held the old woman by a pair of once-strong shoulders under her thin winter jacket. I smelled distillates off her neck. After a life in a hospital maybe they were there for good. Her zipper cut at my chin where I had the stiches removed.

"Are you strong enough?" she said. "To come see him?"

"Can I see her?"

"Well. They're taking care of her. Yes, you can."

They left me alone and all I could see was that what we call the person looms so large when it goes so permanently away. I went back with Greta and we saw through the glass. He had coal black hair, and a sharp nose. A blanket was around him and he was starting with nothing, with me.

"Can I come back?" I said to Greta, and her old strained eyes stayed on me.

"You come back whenever you are ready and I'll be right here with him the whole time."

She came with me to the car.

I could think of no name, after all my christenings of creatures. I had him at Argyle's but I found the place a little lonesome. He never cried. I expected a learning difficulty but he would laugh and kick. That seemed healthy enough. My brother Matthew, the Mountie from out west, had his little redhead here one summer. The little guy was testing his father by inching a full glass of milk toward the table's end. "Ta ta," said his father but the redhead pushed the glass further. "Ta ta," said his father firmly. The boy waited, then moved the glass a bit more. "Ta Fucking, Ta!" screamed his old man.

Tata's a name. Yes, of the buses in India. "What's wrong, kid? Nothing to be sad about? Laugh, then. Laugh or I'll call ya Tata." A rainstorm struck and from Argyle's I watched it peel snow from my hill. My two tracks appeared and from here they looked to be almost to the house. She'd had quite the good view of me over here. I let go of the curtain and returned to volume XLIX of the Five Feet, *Beo* . . . expletive . . . *wulf!* The last book! In the fall I had put a drive on, but did not finish all as I had wished — before New Years, before the baby. After *Beowulf*, all that was left was typing up my father's, *Beginning and End of It All*. I pulled that out: *When I was growing up, I always felt lonely and I had a hard time with it. When I went to leave for the war, there was too much drift ice for the Aspy to sail. I had to go home and say goodbye to my parents all over again. I remember seeing how happy my mother's face was to see me back on the doorstep.* I read of his being crowded on a ship with other Canadian men, approaching by night his first point of battle. Then I could read no more of this right now. There was Tim's letter, at the end of the *Book of Trees*. He wanted his kids only to have that place. Ah, the loose ends in life. All we can do is tie off as many as we can.

I spoke on the phone with Marie in Sydney. She was calling a lot. I walked out to the front of the house and looked up. Broken clouds sailed over the peak, bunching before venturing for a wild white-capped sea. I, or the road, was up a hundred and seven feet; twenty more would see me below Charlie's ledge. I had shovelled three days to get to the tracks properly. I should have waited. The sun melted all that work and more.

I banged the side of the pick against bagged cement. I picked frozen gravel. I turned to see the meandering tracks pass by the apple tree and disappear into snow out of the sun. I expected the meander to move when I would look away then turn back. Such is the effect of twists in roads. And then, like a snap of the fingers, I was up on the flat outside my backdoor. Flat? What a concept. I massaged my lower back not because it ached but because it had so often ached, down on the hill.

In gentle steps I moved over fresh grout that locked in the stones of Smokey. I got down on my knees, the aluminum level showed its bubble between the lines. Mud on shoes would be no matter exiting and entering automobiles, for there would be no mud. In your dry sneakers you could go from Rocket to house to Rocket, which would not be the case, as the transmission failed coming home from the hospital. I now had Argyle's car, 'the Locket'.

From miles and miles around folks showed up to see the road. It became the spring thing to do. They waved for me to come down to talk to them about the hill and all said the same thing: "You got her done!" People wouldn't use it. They had for so long not tried the hill that to stay at the bottom was ritual.

"You probably can't turn up there, anyway! And we'll have to back her down! Yalp, no doubt!" They surely thought this. The road frightened them; it always had. Lay a carpet to a jungle where only good lions roar and people will approach on the side, with guns. Who knew what to expect if you attempted the hill? There was all that talk up there with Miles MacPherson. And, mufflers, brakes, don't forget, were everything in the Highlands. No. Sorrowful circumstance brought them that spring. The road was a convenient topic.

Argyle had written a letter I carried. Sun warmed the stone behind the house to create a bit of an oven. It's true that for months this place stays in darkness but when spring arrives the sun hits from the sea first thing in the morning and the last place to get evening light in all the village is here. I see the village wait in darkness an hour before sun leaves here. The envelope had a quotation: "At the End of Your Road".

I touched the bridge of my glasses. I tasted cement when I bit to remove a glove. I spat an envelope corner and dug a dirty finger through a sharp seam. Alongside the drying grout of Smokey stone, I rested an arm on the rough spruce siding of the house. I flapped open the page. I filled my rib cage with sea air when a big drop struck me in the eye. Fir, dripping from talons, Gaita. I waited till he was gone:

I'm either there. Or, you're reading this. If you have my boy, my soul's at peace. A boy, yes, I didn't tell you. I also didn't tell you that the doctor advised me to have surgery to remove the baby. General anesthesia is one thing. But, and I can't tell you exactly why, of all things I needed to be present for this. I am stubborn. But the little bugger wants out so I'm off to the hospital tonight. I don't feel good. My constitution was never strong in around my periods; nothing was ever regular. It was the diabetes. It was maybe other things. Only we know our bodies. I expected the worse because of what that doctor in town said. I saw Greta Daisley, a retired nurse from down north who used to be midwife. I saw her in her home and she said I had to watch it, that I was older and I had my condition. She had told me a long while back when I went to see her that if ever I got pregnant I would really have to watch it. So I never planned to. And then I was in my forties so that was that, anyway. Till I met with you, and then guess what the frig happens. I was ready, though, from the get-go. I didn't want to even whisper about my constitution. I felt I'd be chancing it even mentioning it. But to have a child. Of my own. I didn't allow myself to think it. I was barren I figured so I blocked out any hope. Which we do, one way or another, to survive. This was real though and it was happening to me. Greta told me to see the doctor. He confirmed I had thin walls and suggested, considering at least, aborting. That wasn't going to happen.

No, I ignored all hope of ever finding someone. I saw you at the bank one day, in with the manager consolidating your loans and you said hello to me as you were leaving. You looked so alone. Then, I was way at the back of the church when your father died and you played. I heard you across the water for years. We all did. I just wanted to be company and be a friend mainly. Tim was your friend and that must have been hard. It was some fun tying that bracelet to old broken-wing. I knew you had him. Mom said you stole him from the property but that was okay because he used to fly back to her and keep her company.

I feel in the end anything can happen to anyone. You just keep waking, keep going about it. I suppose you taught me that. If it does turn out you have no one after me, you just go on doing what you do up on that hill. Build your road, read your red books, feed the crows. You were doing all right up there after that hard time you had overseas. I hope I respected that. They said that maybe you needed a psychologist with that quest for your glasses and that taking on of that road. I knew you were just occupying your mind and I learned soon enough that no one need worry. That you were as tough as an old cherry tree. I'm not saying to always go on living like that forever but it is some accomplishment if you do. To put on fires when you want, dig in the ground, build with logs and stone. See all you see up there, of nature and the ocean, and the seasons come and the storms hit, while teetering on a hill. Who isn't teetering, on their own hill, anyway?

Best thing to have is another. You were no puzzle. No hermit, no hater of people. Shy, maybe. But the opposite's true always, isn't it? Keep it small like Charlie, just go for the crumbs. Keep that stew on the back of your woodstove. Throw in the odd turnip as required. And take care of the child if he sees the light of day. I hope you get your road done.

No signature. I adjusted my glasses and looked below at the hill. A big salty tear and not from any fir crown fell, others followed like railcars leaving a track. I spoke into them, "Tears, now?" But my shoulders rose and my glasses got splashed. I was so tired of it all. I took the glasses off and wiped them in my shirttail when upon the bank, you would never believe who was there, on his ledge, shifting on account of lameness, turning prettily away from me, lifting and starting a trot upland. He passed through his high cover of birch, beech, and maple, till higher and higher he went out of sight and I never saw him again.

Greta Daisley called. "I'm sorry, Miles. I forgot to tell you that one of the girls on duty that night said she wanted him called, "Smokey", be it boy or be it girl. Wait. Am I wrong? Was it Hazel?" He was at my feet in a bassinet, looking up. I saw my mother's coal-black eyes, I saw my father's sharp nose and Argyle's small sad smile so I had lots of company.

It was the time, it was the place for "Goodbye Old Loneliness".

> *Goodbye old loneliness*
> *I have found someone new*
> *Goodbye old loneliness*
> *She's better than you.*

CPSIA information can be obtained
at www.ICGtesting.com
Printed in the USA
LVOW07s0516101116
512357LV00001B/5/P